THE WORLD AND THE ZOO

A SHORT NOVEL

ROB ROENSCH

Outpost19 | San Francisco
outpost19.com

Roensch, Rob
The World and The Zoo/ Rob Roensch
ISBN 978-1-944853-67-9 (pbk)

Library of Congress Control Number: 2019957148

The World and The Zoo by Rob Roensch is part
of the ongoing Short-ish series of novellas and
extended essays, published by Outpost19. Learn
more at outpost19.com/Shortish.

OUTPOST19

ORIGINAL PROVOCATIVE READING
SAN FRANCISCO | @OUTPOST19

again,
for Carrie and Tully and Penny

"Foxes have dens and birds have nests,
but the son of man has no place to lay his head."

Luke 9:58

THE WORLD AND THE ZOO

In the spring before graduation, I began to lose my sense of time. I mistook this feeling at first for freedom, and even joy. More than once I woke up in the dark and didn't know if the world was still holding off morning or had become the next evening without me. I remember nothing of the essays I generated to complete the last necessary credit hours and not much more than isolated impressions from the evenings—a chaos of voices and faces—that were then what I and everyone else seemed to believe was the best possible way to live.

The last night, we bought from someone's guy in the Chick-Fil-A parking lot. Later, there was a backyard lit by strings of Christmas lights, a thunderstorm. In an apartment with a seven-thousand-dollar TV and a broken bathroom mirror, a sly dark-lipped girl in red stripes didn't believe me that I could slice into my own thumb with a kitchen knife, or maybe just wanted to see if I would.

Around three, a stranger appeared in his sleek rented graduation robe for a joke, but then I saw it was someone I knew. In a sticky dark kitchen, promises I don't remember were made.

I also don't remember how I got back to my apartment.

For whatever reason, I didn't immediately go inside to pass out.

I discovered the face of my thumb was bleeding again, so I wrapped it in the bottom of my T-shirt and squeezed hard, so it hurt.

I stood in the parking lot listening to the silence of lights left on in other people's apartments and it was like waking up from a dream and finding myself on a path halfway through a dark forest.

I mean to be honest. I know I am not a rebel or an artist or a monk. I will not, in the end, renounce or escape my upbringing.

I grew up outside Dallas. My father is a lawyer. His most frequent client develops technology for use in increasingly surreal techniques for extracting oil and natural gas from vast impure deposits deep beneath the surface of the earth. My mother grew up with some money, as she says, and studied art history and now serves on the boards of several arts organizations. They attend charity galas and golf tournaments and have serious conversations on the phone about preparations for charity galas and golf tournaments. They are capable, even exceptional people; they are even now only mildly and temporarily disappointed in me.

There was and is a space in their world carved out for me. All I had to do to enter it was complete the hours of a day, then the days of a week, then the weeks of a month, then the months of a year, and so on. My grades were good overall and my personal statement had been polished by a helpful man in a tucked-in University polo at the career center who circled words with a pen silver as a mirror. His final verdict on my statement was, "You really make sure to say what employers want to hear."

My father helped secure for me an offer of a paying year-long internship in an elegant silver building, experience that would have been very attractive on law school applications and in the planned future.

But there were questions I needed to answer and I didn't even know what they were. I chose an unpaid summer at the zoo.

3

In the parking lot of the zoo there are grackles. In certain angles of light, there is a subtle blue sheen to the black feathers on their heads; otherwise they are deeply unpleasant. Their eyes are flat. Their beaks are crooked, like overgrown fingernails. They sound like malfunctioning appliances. Across the pavement in twos and threes they spastically stalk insects, bits of blown trash, nothing. On branches overhead they perch, nosy and uncertain.

I found myself noticing them in a new way as I settled my bike into the rack on my first day at the zoo. They had been familiar presences in parking lots large and small, in landscapes weedy and unsettled and landscapes groomed weekly, and so usually blended into the blur of daily life. But, because of the fact that I was going to work at a zoo, a structure designed to confine animals for the purpose of observation, the idea of an animal living so freely just outside (as well as, I would discover, inside, among the lions and gorillas even) seemed for the first time noteworthy.

I watched one for a few moments, tried to absorb his pointy lack of grace, imagined what it would feel like to jerk-walk over hot pavement with feet made of a few long scaly fingers, each tipped with a claw.

My last semester, one day not long after Donald Trump's inauguration, my friend Bryce was driving us through campus and we stopped at a red light next to a cop who had pulled over a beat-up green pickup and was standing over a man he'd handcuffed. The man sitting on the curb was Hispanic, wearing thick overalls stained at the cuffs and across the chest with black grease, like he'd come directly from some difficult heavy work. He was staring into the pavement between his feet. Bryce gave me this look, this bare nod, this unfamiliar tight, triumphant smile.

"Once his ass gets sent back to Mexico," he said, "he's not coming back."

Bryce had never said anything like that to me before. I didn't know what to say.

"Maybe," I managed and felt untethered. I pretended to respond to a text I hadn't received. Then I looked out the window at girls walking past on their way to class and imagined their names and let the feeling dissipate, to my shame.

But in the summer, at the zoo, I thought about that moment often: sitting on a bench facing the tiger enclosure, crunching through a handful of almonds one by one, watching the tiger stalk the boundary of his enclosure, back and forth, following the path his instincts had worn in the earth. He had a round, strong face, like Bryce. "You asshole," I thought. Then I thought, what kind of loser silently insults a tiger?

I enjoyed watching giraffes eat. Their tongues are blue-black and powerful and, together with their lips, operate with surprising sensitivity, more like a hand and wet fingers than like the much weaker human tongue and lips.

Giraffes are of course known most for their height, but as a giraffe, would you think of yourself as tall? All animals, even the strangest to us, know themselves as normal.

It's very difficult to consider an animal without getting stuck in your own human body's expectations.

The giraffe's height alone does not make imagining what it would feel like to be a giraffe interesting; what does is the distance between the creature's soul-brain—which must center in its sensitive lips and tongue—and the earth. Your attention is most often in the trees, much like a bird. How unusual it would be to see a giraffe watching its own feet as it walked. Like them we trust the earth is always beneath us.

I slept in a one-bedroom apartment with yellow walls in a modestly hip central Oklahoma City neighborhood. It had been rented for the year by a friend of one of my friends who moved to New York who had also moved to New York; he had it rented through August; no one bothered asking me to pay the few months' rent.

The zoo was well north and west of the apartment. Since I was alone in the city, and had not accepted my father's attempted bribe of a new leased car if I abandoned the zoo, I had no car to drive there in. To take a bus required too much waiting, and would have made me trace over and over the rut of an inelegant shape on a map of the city and in my own brain, and would have invited comment from my father. I had a bike at college, a good bike; I'd used it maybe four times. The bike became the only way.

I didn't intend to enjoy biking to and from work. As I biked outward through the neighborhood of the yellow rooms, I could observe what life had been lived while I was elsewhere. In the afternoons, unmown lawns were mown; on Monday mornings, neat porches were now messy: shifted chairs, empty beer cans on the stairs. The leaves of shade trees shimmered in my ears in the wind.

I do own a helmet but I couldn't make myself wear it. It would have been like swimming wrapped in plastic.

The street cross-town was more spacious but also more trafficked. I had to take the overpass over the highway and so could also keep an eye on the construction of the new interchange, the array of heavy yellow machines and white pickups standing sentry around fields of unpeeled earth, burnt-orange bare muscle. Then I passed oddly shaped bureaucracy centers—a sandstone castle from the future for Oklahoma Public Health, the blue-windowed OKSA, a library distribution center with windows narrow as a prison's. There was a barbeque place in what was maybe an old Pizza Hut, a squat square daycare with a mural of hand-drawn slightly off-kilter Sesame Street characters. When I turned north, I entered what seemed to be empty, slightly-rolling grassland, and then there was the first steeple, a Baptist church, then a Seventh Day, a Church of Christ, another Baptist, a Nazarene, and, on a corner where you can see the highway, something called Waypoint that has a sleek sign that could also be used to advertise a waterslide park.

It's as if every empty space in Oklahoma City will one day be occupied by a church and a parking lot with enough spots for every member of the choir to park their own white SUV or pickup. On weekday dawns their parking lots are as empty as everywhere else.

At the last light before the zoo there is an old gas station with a beautiful oversized swooping rusting chevron sign, bird-in-flight-like, from when gas stations meant the possibility of freedom, not price comparisons, obligatory commutes, and war.

The conference room I was directed to on my first day at the zoo was, upon first glance, not unlike a college classroom—an array of familiar tiny-desked chairs, a white board with marker smears, a wall of closed windows, a few young men and women my age with their faces pointed into their phones—so I was at first disappointed. I couldn't help but wonder if this room was merely a slightly different kind of nowhere.

I didn't take a chair but went to the window. Outside there were thick cottonwoods and also, I saw, a long ordinary chainlink fence and, beyond that fence, another long chainlink fence—a double layer. I was looking into the back of an animal enclosure—I would learn later that it was the okapi enclosure. I couldn't see any animals through the thick growth, but I knew they were there. And there were grackles, too visible, stabbing at the earth and air and complaining.

And the room didn't smell like a classroom, I noticed, if I concentrated. I would come to know the smell well enough to not notice it unless I insisted on noticing—grassy, moist, rotting and fresh fruit, earth and shit—the smell of the life of the zoo.

I've always had lots of friends, so at the zoo I decided not to. During the morning break of the orientation, I was vague when asked about my reasons for working at the zoo for free. This was easy enough because I didn't have an articulable answer, and every other new intern had an answer both sensible and vibrant that triggered cascades of questions and anecdotes that filled up the time. One grew up with horses, another had just gotten back to "the states" from research for her thesis project on the Costa Rican ecosystem, another had already been volunteering with the ring-tailed lemurs. They were hardworking biology majors who had fiercely held opinions about brands of notebooks, enjoyed cold-weather camping, made their own energy drinks.

On the tour in the open-air tram, they chattered happily among themselves about graduate schools and I listened and decided I wouldn't like to have to go to graduate school to get a job at a zoo. It was like only being allowed to enter a house after spending three years studying doorknobs.

It was on this tour that I first saw Caroline.

Caroline, like many zoo employees, was wearing a wide straw hat against the sun; hers was fraying, and she always wore it tipped further back than most, so, she told me later, she could actually see what was going on with the sky. She was my age, freckled and long-haired and not immediately lovely, though she was, and very much so; my first thought about her was: I bet she can run very fast. She was leaning against the wide doorway of the gift shop shed outside Big Cat Forest, watching the world go past. She waved at us in an ironic way, waving without really waving; I was the only one who waved back, and without meaning to.

After the tour we returned to the classroom for paperwork and short films about reporting sexual harassment and what to do about blood. It may as well have been in the back room of a Target.

Then a woman like a cheerful linebacker entered the classroom with a red-tailed hawk perched on her thick yellow leather glove. It had a claw for a face. I was enchanted. Here it was, the real world.

The others looked up; I took a step forward, looked into the center of the hawk's black eye and had the experience I have often with an animal of not being acknowledged but wanting to be.

"This here's Shadow," said the woman with the hawk on her glove to all of us. "She'd be more than happy to tear out your heart."

Late one unreasonably warm Tuesday night the previous winter I felt my phone buzz and realized it didn't buzz and I looked out the window and saw it was much windier than I had known and in the same minute realized I was well and truly baked but also oddly awake, and my roommates were just going to keep murdering aliens all night, so I might as well be productive.

I went into my room with my laptop in the dark and ticked open all the tabs I'd filed into a bookmark folder called "Later."

It was necessary to not stop and think.

Most internship applications allowed for mindless repetition: copy-and-paste, fiddle with personal statement, allow automatic field fill-in, attach resume. I didn't realize the zoo internship application was for the zoo until I got to the question about why I wanted to work at the Oklahoma City Zoo. I didn't remember why I'd found and saved the zoo application in the first place.

I filled it out; words moved through me, frictionless. I saw out the window of my dark room a bare branch bending gently in the steady wind like a finger being pulled back, and wondered for a moment how an owl's life was different on windy night. I wish I could say I wrote about the owl but I don't remember what I wrote.

The woman who carried the hawk was named Maggie, and she was one of the supervisors of the Animal Care interns. She treated us and the animals the same. She was so pleased to see anyone eating, human or animal, that she would vocally approve of what was being eaten to the eater: "You dig that melon in the morning, yeah?" "You and those peanut butter and jellies, good energy in that!" She called every animal by a first name that was not listed anywhere and was also not universally understood by the rest of the staff. Many of the names sounded like the real names of grandmothers and grandfathers: Edith the gorilla; Alvin the black bear. If the animals in question were too numerous to be named, like in the little room full of fluttering bats, she called them "girls." She drank at least three cans of Coke a day.

After lunch (I was the only intern who took a roast beef wrap, not vegetarian, from the tray) there was a short film, so old that by the time it had been digitized it was already flickering and faded in places, about the history of the Oklahoma City Zoo. The video was mainly about the names of people who had paid for exhibits and renovations. Some of the names were vaguely familiar because, I realized, they were also the names of downtown streets. Maybe, I saw, even the zoo was just another piece of the world to be bought and sold. But at least there was a marvelous photograph of Judy, the zoo's first elephant on her wedding day in a wedding veil that was "waterproof," which made good sense. I also appreciated the story from the summer of 1938 about the black bear scheduled to be slaughtered and served at a feast for zoo donors who was saved by the city's penny-collecting children, and so donated to the zoo and given the name "Barbeque Bear" which is not unlike giving your child the name "YouAlsoWillOneDayDie."

We were gathering our materials at the end of the day to leave when Maggie dashed back in the room, which was not itself odd—already she was the sort of person who dashed into rooms—but her face was blank, like she was afraid, and she didn't say anything. She was followed shortly by a lanky, big-handed college basketball-coach-on-TV type in a blue suit, with a tie that was a lion silhouetted against the sunset. In contrast to Maggie's obvious anxiety, he was calm, and smiling like an uncle.

"Is this the latest crop?" he said. "Good looking group."

"You'll have to wait," said Maggie, tremblingly, to us. "You can't leave yet."

"Why?" said a woman my age in a complicated and unnecessary red raincoat and mud-caked hiking boots. I knew she was on her way to Stanford in the fall because she'd mentioned it to the group five times.

"Now what I'm about to tell you shouldn't leave this room," said the TV coach, the boss, still smiling, to all of us. "Do you understand?"

"That depends," said the red raincoat.

"Do you understand?" he said, still smiling, to her. "Yes."

"Now our zoo has been experiencing over the past few years, a phenomenon of animals, shall we say, disappearing." At the word "disappearing" he fluttered his fingers in the same way as you would to mock a television magician.

"I've never heard about that," said the red raincoat.

"That's right. Because no one who works here talks about it. If word got out, that could complicate our jobs and," he said, opening his hands, "make it much more difficult to find and recover the animals."

"He was just a baby. Lemurs need keeper attention, and their mothers," said Maggie, on the edge of tears. The coach shot her a look, but Maggie was too distraught to notice. "What if he never learns to climb?"

"How many animals are missing?" said red raincoat.

"All you need to know is that we've instituted a new security protocol. So Keeper Haberstram, here, will need to check your belongings on your way in and out of the compound each day."

"I'm not letting anyone go through my stuff," said the red raincoat. "I know my rights."

"There's your rights and there's the conditions of your employment. If you'd like to spend the summer making fundraising calls, that can be arranged. You can just let your supervisor know." The young woman in the red raincoat could only stand there, blinking. The boss ran a hand through his hair, spoke something to himself in his head that produced a smile. He took a moment to look around the room, let each of us meet his eyes. "I don't mean to start off on the wrong foot," he said. "I'm happy you're here. My name is Anthony Colcord." (I recognized the name from the zoo-history film—the now defunct Colcord African Plains Outlook.) "I'm the operations manager here and Vice President of the foundation. Please don't hesitate to let me know what questions or problems you encounter over this summer. Improving the quality of the zoo experience for all is my most essential goal. It goes without saying that if you see something, or hear something about any of the missing animals, you will let me know. And call me Anthony. Any other questions?"

There were none.

"Then I'll leave you to it," he said, and smiled, and left.

"Who would steal a lemur?" said another intern.

"A little sedative," said Maggie, sadly, "and she'd fit into a handbag." She choked back a sob.

I could imagine it. Walking out through the zoo gates into the parking lot with, stuffed in my old worn green school backpack, a map of Oklahoma City, half a bottle of warm Dr. Pepper, a dreaming lemur.

Growing up, I had no more meaningful experiences with zoos than any other child in my sort of life. The zoo was for the occasional summer weekend, the end-of-year elementary school field trip on a hot gray day. Zoos were a mild sort of magic, not unlike getting a new video game. Something to enjoy and forget.

The only zoo experience I had that broke through into any sort of wonder came late, on our high school trip to Washington, DC. After a morning acting properly mournful at Arlington, we were scheduled for several hours at the National Zoo. We were dropped off, given instructions on when to reassemble at the hippos, and let go.

The novelty of partial freedom so far away from home was intoxicating, much more so than the promise of struggling to see where the cheetah was hiding in the corner, watching lions sleep, reading plaques of facts about poisonous frogs. We split into the usual packs, chattering so fast and loud it felt like singing.

I ended up with a handful of my friends in an exhibit on river ecology. Odd ducks, a vat of eels. At one point you could enter a cave (impossible-to-see bats, coiled patterned snakes) and then find yourself in a concrete hallway beneath a blue-green glass ceiling. I paused there behind my friends a moment because the light was peculiar and it took me a moment to see why—because the light was underwater light, but I was dry. As I understood this over my head, in the river, two otters, brown sleek spirits, whipped toward me along the current and past and, as I watched, curved and returned, to me, the pair of them, and they spun whip-quick circles in the water above my head. Perhaps it was only because I was tall enough for them to notice my head through the glass; perhaps I reminded them of the man who slid them morsels of fish.

It was like a vision, but it was real: the whirling otters above my head close enough and impossible to touch.

All the interns were supposed to meet at the elephant habitat the morning of the second day and I thought I knew where I was going, but I did not.

Caroline was just opening up the little gift shop shed. She was wearing the straw hat. She was also wearing, I saw, plain and well-scuffed running sneakers.

"You know which way I go to the elephants?" I said.

"There's a map by the mountain lion statue," she said, without turning. It seemed like she should have had a country accent, but she didn't. I felt, like a tiny shock, that I wanted to see her face.

"Can't you just tell me? I'm new."

She fit a hook on one of the swinging doors into the wall, securing it, before turning up to me.

"Are you really lost, or are you just trying to talk to me?" she said.

"Yes," I said. "And I'm late."

"There's a map literally right there," she said, pointing over my shoulder. "And there's signs everywhere."

"I always miss signs," I said.

"I'm Caroline," she said.

"Zack," I said.

"The quickest thing to do would be to go right through the tigers," she said. "Keep going until you see the giant ugly temple. That's what you want."

"Thanks," I said. "I'll see you later."

"Good luck," she said, though it wasn't clear about what.

It was on the walk to the elephants that I first spotted Doc, one of the senior keepers, a neatly white-bearded man, all elbows and knees, squatting and poking at something in the dirt just inside the okapi enclosure, grimacing like an about-to-retire homicide detective in a movie.

"Goddamn San Diego," he said, though he was alone, apparently in conversation with the rest of the world.

Inside the zoo, you understand how strange it is that we live our days surrounded by squirrels. You wonder how they don't fear the lions and the wild dogs, and you wonder for the first time why they don't fear you. You see them as themselves, not as background. You notice how they move vertically up and down tree trunks with the confidence of a person walking across a room. In towering branching canopies they see ordinary paths through the world.

I deleted Netflix from my phone, but I did sometimes check on the YouTube accounts that upload videos of young maybe Russian men on trespassing walks in ordinary sneakers along the edges of the rooftops of tremendously tall buildings, across the exposed steel beams of skyscrapers under construction. The videos are difficult and almost painfully pleasurable to watch. A tiny video on a screen the size of a hand somehow allows you to share in a moment of real danger, a feeling of infinite space opening up all around you; you also are alone in the sky.

That Friday I got stuck raking out the red panda enclosure at the end of the day and got back late and when I walked into the locker room it was chaos—all the lockers had been opened, as if by an earthquake, and Maggie and Doc and a handful of other keepers were pawing through the open mouths of the interns' backpacks while the interns waited against the wall on the other side of the room.

Anthony Colcord, standing in the center of the room to oversee, whipped his head around to note my presence and, then, instead of saying anything, watched me.

"What's going on?" I said.

"What do you know about the Tokay gecko?" he said.

"Is that the one that regrows its own tail? If you tear it off?"

"You got it, kid," said Doc, his hands inside someone's many-zippered canvas bag. Anthony Colcord turned back to watch the search.

They didn't find any trace of the newly missing gecko in the backpacks, or anywhere else.

On that evening's bike ride back to the yellow apartment, I imagined what it would feel like to lose an arm.

It is easier to ride a bicycle with no hands, provided you maintain a certain speed, than it is to steer with only one.

I had always needed an alarm to wake up, but I found I did not need an alarm for the zoo. Is very different to wake up only because the room has become bright. An alarm reminds you about your responsibilities, but watery early morning brightness has nothing to do with you. The world can be experienced not as a set of tasks to be completed, but as a lake to choose to enter.

By the second week I felt oddly at home, which was ridiculous because I was so temporary when I told Maggie my last name was spelled wrong on my nametag she said it didn't matter. The map of the zoo was barely penciled into my brain, and I still had to rely on arrows on signs, though I at least knew where the signs were.

That Tuesday, because of the threat of storms, the crowds were thin; word was the summer camps all cancelled. The few visitors were neon-raincoated and hooded, puffy slow-moving flamingos.

I was on my way to the elephant enclosure in a spattering rain to help with some fence repair by the lake when the wind shifted and there was a marvelous crack of lightning and the closest shelter was Caroline's gift shop shed.

She was sitting on a milk crate, hatless, wet-haired, leaning against the ice cream case like she could fall asleep against it, looking out into the world.

"You scared of thunder?" she said as I entered, not turning to me.

"I'd be out in it if I could be," I said, which was sort of true. "But they said take shelter if there's lightning. So that's what I'm doing."

"I hope you're not one of those people who says they love watching storms," she said. Her voice was flat, impossible to read. I took off my hat and shook it out, slicked my hair back, then put it back on. I took only a moment to observe the interior of the gift shop. There were key chains and bumper stickers and a spinning rack of postcards. Candy bars for two dollars each. Five-dollar umbrellas for fifteen dollars. A wall of shelves of tiny stuffed tigers and, for some reason, penguins, even though there were no penguins at the zoo. Someone— Caroline—had arranged the tigers and penguins in an alternating pattern.

"You get sick of sitting here all the time?" I said.

"Sometimes," she said. "I read."

"It would drive me crazy," I said.

"I need the money," she said. "They sometimes give me overtime."

"I don't get paid," I said.

"So you don't need the money," she said.

"Being paid would be nice," I said.

"You want to be a zookeeper?" she said. "You got it all planned?"

"No," I said. "I'm trying to figure it out."

She looked at me then.

"You're spending all summer interning for free for a job you don't want just to figure it out? That sounds nice," she said.

"It's not all nice," I said. "I mean, my apartment doesn't even have wifi." She laughed. "Okay," I said. "I guess that sounds stupid."

"You want a crate?" she said. "There's another behind the register."

"I'm not supposed to stay long," I said.

"Suit yourself," she said.

I got the crate and sat beside her.

For graduation, my friend Bryce received a new car as a gift. He was not someone who I had identified as having an especially large amount of money in his family, though neither did he struggle. Like me, he had never had a part-time job. He was the sort of kid grown-ups called "young man"—he did student government, participated in the day-of-service volunteer opportunities and campus clean-ups I did not participate in and wore the T-shirts when we played pick-up basketball. I remember him once carrying a passed-out mutual friend down three flights of stairs like his giant baby.

He was planning to spend the summer before UT law school at a prestigious state government internship program that would send him to D.C. and who knows where else.

At the after-graduation party he had us all sit in his new car, leaving our beers on the sidewalk. The car was a BMW, not unlike my father's car. It smelled not only new but somehow smooth, as if it was edible.

"Listen," he said, and started the car. Booming, buttery layers of hip-hop erased the outside world. "Check this out," he said, looked at me in the passenger seat, nodding, and pressed a button. I had no idea what changed inside the car, inside the overwhelming expensive sound, inside the pureness of the blasting cool artificial air. He seemed to think I understood.

"Incredible," I said, though I could not hear my voice.

When I entered the room, Doc was sitting on a folding chair, talking to the sedated river otter in his arms. "It's time to sleep," he said, quietly, but without tenderness. "It's time to sleep now." I didn't want to break the quiet. When he looked up and spotted me he wasn't embarrassed. "You wash your hands before you get your gloves on?" he said. I nodded. He was also wearing long sky-blue gloves pulled up to his elbows.

"So he'll just sleep?"

"How else would we do it?"

"Well, they don't sleep when they do it for real."

"Do I look like a lady otter to you?" he said.

"No," I said.

He hurked himself robotically to his feet, keeping the otter still on the shelf of his arms. He laid him carefully on a dull silver table.

The device to stimulate the prostate to induce ejaculation was also dull silver. Many things in the room were dull silver, and clean, and smelled of bleach.

This is where baby otters come from.

One day a few neatly dressed men with well-combed gray hair stationed themselves at various points around the zoo—the parking lot, the path to the children's area, the tram stop, the entrance to the sea lions—to offer tiny New Testaments to passers-by. I knew they could be kicked off private property, but I also knew it was doubtful that any organization in Oklahoma would, if anyone would even complain in the first place. They were not unfamiliar figures to me—men like them had appeared not infrequently on campus, outside the movie theater and the mall.

I never took an offered New Testament, but I did respect the simplicity and clarity of their mission, and their persistence. What it would feel like to carry a backpack full of words you believed in the heart of your heart were not only beautiful and instructive but saving, and it was your responsibility and your only peace to offer those words to any and every stranger you saw.

When I passed by Caroline's shed I pretended not to look in and then I looked in and she wasn't looking out but was, I was surprised to see, absorbed in one of the little green New Testaments, opened to somewhere halfway through.

I stopped in her doorway. She didn't look up.

"Can I interest you in a tiny penguin?" she said.

"Getting some devotional time in?" I said.

"Are you Christian?" she said.

"I went to Sunday school for awhile," I said.

"I'm not, either," she said. I didn't know what to say. She kept reading.

"My favorite story," I said, "was that part after they capture Jesus with Peter and the cock crowing. How Jesus says, Peter, you're gonna betray me three times, and Peter says, no way, Jesus. And then he does it."

"You mean 'deny,'" said Caroline. "Peter denies him. He doesn't betray him."

"Same difference," I said.

"Not really," she said. "And that's kind of messed up that that's your favorite story. Most people pick, like, the loaves and fishes."

"What's your favorite?"

"The empty tomb," she said quickly. "The very end of Mark, when the women go to visit the dead body and he's not there. They freak out."

"That's dark," I said.

"Says the boy who likes the story about Jesus' best friend selling him out."

"You've got me there," I said.

"I did get you," she said. She looked up finally, smiled. "Sorry, I can be a little crazy." She returned to the book.

Later I saw Doc shooing two neatly dressed gray-haired men with backpacks full of tiny New Testaments past the parrots toward the exit. He was using the same gestures—arms extended, open hands—that he used to encourage the llamas to return to their stall in the evening.

I wouldn't have believed the amount of time I would spend shoveling shit but it only makes sense. Shoveling shit is part of life, and also part of our usual pretending about what life is and is not, since the reason we shoveled so much shit every single day is so it didn't seem to zoo visitors that animals shit so much.

There was a dedicated shovel or two or three in every enclosure as well as a specific and unlabeled place where the shovel must be replaced to, a fact I discovered the first time I helped Doc prep the rhino enclosure. It had been a busy early morning clearing debris and downed branches from the expanse of pounded down earth after a windy night. My forearms were buzzing from the chainsaw. I had a scrape on my neck. Overhead the clouds were insane, racing, like two hands had pulled apart the cotton of the sky and dropped it into a great stream.

"Kid!" I heard. And there was Doc, with a bandana around his neck that gave him the aura of an ancient golden retriever, glaring at me.

"What?" I said. He was holding one of the shit shovels. He pointed at it. "First rule. You put tools back where you found them. God damn it." Putting the shit shovel in the wrong place, I would learn, was exactly the sort of thing that made him angry. There was a right way to care for things, even shit shovels.

What I also learned: elephant shit was heavy, and there was a lot of it, as only makes sense. The carnivore shit smelled the worst and had the consistency of sticky black congealed blood. The shit of animals that eat a lot of plants smelled more like the essence of grassy earth, like gardens.

I scrubbed my hands and arms as rigorously as I was told to, but the smell didn't wash completely away, even in the wind, even in dreams.

I decided to dedicate myself to conscious contemplative observation of animal life. If I was going to seek real questions and real answers, if was going to see through the surface of the world to the greater truths, it only made sense that I should make a practice of total selfless attention.

One dull thick afternoon, I sat on a bench to watch, at length, a gorilla pick its nose. What did I learn? A gorilla's finger is much like my finger, but fatter and grayer. A gorilla's nose is more integrated into its face than my nose is, so to pick it is a slightly more intimate act.

Such observations did not exactly instantly add up to the secret name of God.

"How would you steal a stork?" said Maggie.

"What?"

"I keep trying to work it out," she said. We were digging out a weedy part of the ditch in the giraffe enclosure. I was surprised how much of my job turned out to involve work that was mainly landscaping for animals who did not care. The giraffes weren't out, but the storks who shared the enclosure were nerding around here and there, darting their long beaks into the grass after whatever unlucky beetle. The storks were a wonderful combination of sly beauty—the slant of their eyes and the needle of their beaks and the usual useful grace of wings—and aesthetic error—the spindly, out-of-proportion traffic-cone orange of their legs. I found I admired and even envied them. They didn't need us; to them, we were walking barren trees.

It would be easier, I thought, to steal a bird than it would be to steal an animal that tracked you as something to fear or something to maybe eat.

To steal a stork, I thought, maybe you just waited for the moment and snatched it up by its spindly legs. You could carry one upside-down in each hand, like experimental folding chairs.

"It wouldn't be impossible, I guess," I said. "I mean, when Doc sedated that otter it was, like, a giant furry slug."

"It's not the animals themselves that would be the hard part," she said. "It's getting past the people. Even without the bag search. Think about it: you notice if someone's carrying a bag they usually don't have, right?

Or if their backpack looks a little full? And I keep tabs on that. I watch. I've got good eyes."

"Well, you can't see through the back of your head," I said, and she paused, considered, then turned her head as far as she could to the left, forced her eyes all the way to the left, made a mental note, then to the right the same.

"There's less than ninety degrees I can't see," she said, twisted back to normal. "And I can always move my feet."

"That's true," I said. "It's too bad we weren't more closely descended from owls."

She laughed, a quick bark.

"I'd rather be able to move my eyes than be able to stare at my own bottom," she said.

I tried to imagine twisting my head as far as it could go, and then twisting it further. Our bodies didn't have to be what they are. We are so limited by what we get used to. We think the world is made only of certain colors because that's what we can see.

Watching the storks poke the knives of their beaks into grass I caught myself thinking "unlucky beetle," but it makes no sense to call a beetle lucky or unlucky; insects, I've always felt but never articulated to myself until the zoo, don't have individual voices, only a collective species hum. The inside of a beehive is one buzzing. What does it matter to a collective voice if one bee is squashed? The great buzzing of their life is too distributed for the collective to mourn or pause or even notice. In the same way, what does the world care if one person is in pain? if one person vanishes? if one person dies? Ten people? One hundred? One hundred thousand? What does it matter?

I often paused at the beehive with the clear plastic panel to observe for a few moments the frantic order of bee life. Not unlike what cities and traffic look like from the sky.

The size of the world, of the universe, is obliterating.

The question is how to not be drowned by this perspective. The question is how to not only see but feel, and recognize, each person—each driver of each tiny car on the highway thousands of feet below you—as one individual soul, also capable of seeing human life from a great distance, and wondering.

One day I shared what was left of a pack of peanut M&Ms with Caroline and she asked me if I ever went down to Bricktown and I said no and she said she was going to the movies with a friend so after work that's where I went.

I understood by the expression on the face of the cashier at Sonic that I smelled like the zoo, and the bike ride, and the summer.

I took my enormous limeade slush and paper bag of cheeseburger outside.

It was getting towards dusk, but still red-bright out, with a dry hot wind. I sat on a wall near the fountain in front of the movie theater, close enough to feel the spray and smell the chlorine, to eat and watch the summertime evening city walk by.

I'd been spending time surrounded by wandering crowds at the zoo, but the zoo crowd was different from the city crowd. A zoo crowd's collective attention is directed away from itself toward the surrounding animal-displaying-and-concealing landscape. In other words, people go to the zoo to look at animals, not to be in relation to each other, so there is a calm feeling to entering a zoo crowd, the way the jackfish in the center of the school must feel.

A city crowd isn't anxious necessarily, but it is more alert to itself: couples on dates strolling along the canal and pointing out the gliding ducks to each other as third-margarita older folks idly follow their progress from outdoor tables; white families from the suburbs and further out heading from Toby Keith's toward the movies; a sunburned pickup-truck-with-extended-cab father grimly watching over his neon-shorted children; Hispanic families wandering together loosely and absolutely connected; a fat kid in a giant red T-shirt on a mission; young women with sparkles sewn into their jeans and hair billowing expertly in the wind pretending not to know they are being watched; a pack of teenagers with Gatorade bottles full of who knows what, eyes darting everywhere, an aura of feverish mischief left trailing behind.

Watching people was absorbing, not so different from watching animals. In each case you are looking at what is in front of you to see the deeper meaning, what the world truly is. But deep concentration can also be a kind of blindness. I was paying close attention to an old woman in a loose white sweater despite the lingering heat, sitting alone at a table with three other chairs, all pushed out, the table's other places taken by the remains of dinner, plastic baskets full of only ketchup-smeared crumpled napkins. There was a walker set next to her chair; two bright new tennis balls had recently been cut and affixed to the feet of the two front legs. I assumed she had been left to wait for a moment by family members who were, perhaps, purchasing movie tickets or pulling up the car. As I watched her she was in her turn watching a pair of gray pigeons—rock doves—who were picking and squabbling for crumbled bits of ice cream cone around the base of an elegantly shiny black trash can. She had her hands folded on her lap; I could almost imagine her hands were my hands—heavy bony fingers, loose dry paper skin. She was frowning in a restful way. I stared without staring, waiting for a movement, a change in expression.

I didn't notice Caroline until she was standing in front of me. She was accompanied by another girl and I saw (with a quick sinking of my stomach) a boy.

"This is Zachary the future law student," she said by way of introduction.

"It's Zack," I said. "I'm not a law student."

"Yet," she said. "Were you in outer space? I've been saying your name forever." She was wearing a bright white T-shirt and cutoffs. She looked good.

"That's impossible," I said.

"I'm Kaylee," said the girl in an orange OSU tank top, giant mirror sunglasses and without a smile.

"Hey," I said and set what was left of my cheeseburger on the bench, standing up like I had been taught. "I'm Zack."

"And this is my brother, David," said Caroline.

"Of course," I said a little too cheerfully, and I held out my hand to him. David was tall, boy-band-haired, dressed like he'd just come from basketball practice, and really thin. His grip tried too hard.

"You got to intern as a zookeeper?" he said, letting me go. "I thought that was, like, impossible to get."

"It is," said Kaylee.

"Caroline knows way more about the zoo than I do," I said.

"That's not true," she said. "All I know is where things are. You want to come to the movie?"

I did. But I remembered the face of the cashier at Sonic when he'd smelled the zoo on me.

"I've actually got work to do," I said.

"Sounds very important," she said.

"Not really," I said.

"Must be," she said. "So you came all the way down here to say hi?"

"Yeah, I mean, no. I was just, you know, exploring. Thought maybe I'd see you."

"Okay," she said. "Your world. See you tomorrow then?"

"Sure," I said, but she'd already turned. She was lovely, walking away. I never let girls walk away. I always found more words to say. But the words I had seemed wrong, for Caroline.

When I looked back to the old woman there was a pigeon at the tennis-ball feet of her walker. She regarded it with her frowning patient interest. I saw the pigeon was pecking at a little pile of french fries she must have dropped there, to draw close the bird.

There was a quite young pronghorn antelope they were keeping away from the others, in the hospital building, because her mother was sick and couldn't nurse. Maggie called her, "Poor dear," and another keeper said, "poor dear deer" and Maggie said, "poor dear." I was eavesdropping on them while doing inventory on a form on a clipboard —I double-checked the crates of carrots and bruised apples and green or dark leaking bananas; a walk-in freezer full, as always, of great tubes of murky purple horse meat, stacked ice-cold rabbit carcasses. There were racks and racks of frozen mice, little nightmare ice cream scoops.

Maggie and the other keeper talked about the pronghorn's mother: even though I'd been around them for a few weeks and knew Maggie had names for every living creature in her care, it took me a few minutes to understand that "Wilma" was an antelope and not a cantankerous great-aunt.

At a certain point Doc came in. He didn't try to include himself in the conversation or even acknowledge the other keepers. Given my brief encounters with him, it was obvious to me that he would see that talking about animals as if they were people was beneath him. He went directly to some white-board wipe-off charts on the wall full of numbers and abbreviations of words I had not yet sussed out. He tipped his head back to read the information, as if he was wearing glasses, though he wasn't. He was like certain professors, especially the type who lectured in large classes, who only ever spoke directly to students to test if they had done the reading.

"You gave the three-week pronghorn my cocktail?" he said to the room, and Maggie and the other zookeeper shut up. I expected they'd snap back something, but they just looked at each other. I poked my head out to watch.

"We followed the binder?" said the other one, and quietly. "She seemed to take it pretty well."

"That's because she needs more than she's getting," he said and checked his watch. "We can go half this morning, and the evening the full amount. It's always on the wall. There's a difference between the checklist in the binder and the animal at hand."

"Sorry," said Maggie.

Doc didn't answer, but he didn't seem angry, exactly.

I watched as Doc opened up the closest refrigerator, grabbed out a baby's bottle full of what looked like thin yellow milk, slipped it in his armpit. With the bottle under his arm he pulled out another bottle of what looked like bright yellow egg yolk, opened shelves, found a bowl, a bin of white powder. He mixed a pinch of the powder into a few squirts of the egg yolk, whisked it with a fork then took the milk bottle from his armpit, opened and sniffed it, poured half of it away down the sink, tipped in the egg mixture, screwed it tight and shoved it under his arm.

"Why'm I doing this?" he asked me, snapping his head over to catch my eye. I hadn't imagined he would care I was there. "Aren't my armpits full of stink?"

"You're warming it up, right?" I said.

"Good answer," he said. I thought he would say something else, but didn't. I went back to my clipboard in the freezer.

A few minutes later, I heard my name from far away: "Kid." I had to follow the voice a ways down the hall. There was Doc holding the bottle between his palms a few steps from the young pronghorn's cage; it couldn't have been larger than a cat. He didn't turn back to see if I'd come but crouched, swiftly, not like a creaky old man but like a chimp who had made a decision, and shuffled a few feet forward, toward where the antelope was curled, watching. "Hey there girl," he said without inflection. "Hey there." He scooted in closer. She lifted her head, turned away, and he turned her face back to him with a cupped palm and, with a finger to guide, slipped the red rubber milk nipple into the animal's mouth.

"There it is now," he said, and, to me, in the same voice, "you hold the milk like this. Hand underneath. Nice and steady." He was leaning in closer now, whispering. I could see from where I stood that he was blowing gently into her face as she drank.

"My brother once caught this giant black yellow spotted salamander," said Caroline.

"Yeah?" I said. She was on her break, walking with me across the zoo. It was hot. I was carrying to the offices from the elephant enclosure a lunch cooler packed tight with, I'd been told, stool samples. It was heavy enough that I had to remind myself to act like it wasn't heavy.

"Yeah, back before we moved to the city. It was as long as when you spread out your fingers," she said.

"I never caught animals, when I was a kid," I said. I was at tutoring. Or at basketball practice. Or playing video games.

"At first he kept it in this box of dirt, in his room."

"Your parents let him?"

"Yeah they did. Everyone thought it wasn't good for him."

"It's a salamander. It needs to be wet all the time, right?"

"I meant my brother."

"Your brother."

"Yeah, he had leukemia. Has. He shouldn't have even been digging in the dirt in the first place. It's already come back and gone away again. He's on all these crazy drugs."

"So that's why you need the overtime? To help out?"

"What do you think I make at this job?" she said.

"I don't know," I said. "Ten?"

"Let's say I make ten an hour. So that's 350, after taxes. Plus like fifty in time-and-a-half, if I can get it.

How much do you think it costs to, like, go to one of his thousand doctor appointments?"

"I don't know."

"That salamander lived forever. My mom wouldn't let my brother take care of it so I had to. I read up on it. I set it up in this giant cardboard box full of dirt in the garage. I gave it frozen worms. I'd literally dig up the backyard with a shovel to get these worms, super long pink ones, and I'd put them in a bag and throw them in the freezer. When I fed the salamander, I'd cut them up with these specific scissors."

"That's serious. You should be the zookeeper."

"I wouldn't have done it if it was my salamander. It was just for my brother."

When I talked to my father on the phone every Wednesday evening, I could see him in my mind: he was halfway into the second after-dinner scotch, the grooved and foggy glass tucked between stacks of books on the little table next to his reading chair like a hidden object in a puzzle, a clue. He'd just laid down the newspaper or folded over the page he'd gotten to in whatever new book about history the elegant radio voices were murmuring about that week; it was not yet time to give in to the evening and take up the iPad—in the discreet black leather case—to scroll college football arguments and online auctions for old baseball cards. My mother was in the garden, in her studio in the attic, on the phone with her sister. My brother was at basketball practice, pretending to be studying or studying, just as I would have been. The daylight was almost gone, and it was time to honor its passing. It was the time of the evening for conversation.

My father has a respect for traditions, even small ones, too sincere and consistent to dismiss.

And he truly is a good listener. When I was in college, he would ask about what I had been reading and would be more interested in it than I was; because I was working at the zoo he asked about what animals I encountered and what my observations of them were. He complimented me on my focus. He said: "You can't become a good attorney without being able to look and listen."

Initially, of course, he had advised me "with all my heart and mind" to not "throw away a significant opportunity" by working at the zoo. But once my choice was irrevocable (and when I more-or-less agreed to spend the following year as a research assistant at his firm to improve my law school applications) his conversational strategy changed. He allowed me the present in exchange, we both understood, for a shared acceptance of a future.

I told him about the surprising and intricate force of the muscles of a milk snake coiling around my wrist and the interesting psychology of the keeper who worked with the all the big cats who could not bear to so much as look at a spider, even one in a sealed aquarium.

"Any experience can be a value to you, I do believe that," he said. "When I was your age, I was pumping gas on the sly two towns over in the evenings for pocket money, to prove to your mother I could meet her expectations. Now, what many might think is a mindless job is truly an opportunity to practice the work of the mind. I looked closely at the cars; now, I never knew much about cars. But cars are everywhere. They're all around us. There's so much you can learn about people by observing the car they drive. Is it maintained? Do they keep it clean? How do they talk to you? Who is in the car with them? What happens while I'm pumping the gas? How do they say 'thank you'? You assemble these impressions into a picture of a person. There's a great deal you can learn about a person in a few minutes. It's a useful skill, I've found, in my work. You identify who a person is and then you know how to deal with them to get what you want."

The first animals I got to work with independently were the goats in the petting zoo. I monitored their hay and alfalfa supply, their water, scooped up the droppings, made sure their protected corner (with the "Sometimes we need a rest!" sign) was respected.

The goats were like children who didn't know how to talk. Their eyes were pushed out too far to the sides of their heads; some had eyes that were an unsettlingly lovely blue. They stood and chewed while the human children brushed them unnecessarily. They were bristly, gentle. They got few but odd inspirations, like a sudden deep desire to stand on top of a box and remain there, chewing, satisfied. The children patted them too firmly; the parents said to the child "look at the goat!" while the child was already looking at the goat.

One morning toward the end of June there was a piece of paper affixed to the locker-room door by pieces of clear plastic tape exactly the length of the top and bottom of the piece of paper, words typed in bolded letters, each line centered: "MONDAY MORNING MEETING ALL EMPLOYEES MANDATORY." Someone, I saw, had gone to a certain amount of trouble.

I tried to open the door to drop my bag and lunch and grab my gloves and zoo cap and name tag, but the door was locked.

The classroom was packed; the Maintenance guys, in a clump in a corner with their gloves on, relaxed into the chairs and against the wall. Lots of people I'd never talked to. That one short keeper who'd been singing to the skates when we'd gone through on the tour. Maggie and Doc were up front with the rest of the keepers, Doc slightly off to the side as always, Maggie whispering something fiercely so close into the ear of another keeper she could have bitten it off. The interns were in the center of the room and had formed a close circle. One had an insanely bright orange water bottle dangling from a belt loop. Caroline was leaning on the back wall, fraying straw hat held across her chest like a shield; she was neither bored nor interested, merely waiting. She didn't look for me. There was no room in the intern circle, or next to Caroline, so I stood for a moment in the pocket of empty space, but then there was a hand—fingers spread—in my back, pushing me forward a step, gentle enough, though firm, and I took a step in and behind me Anthony Colcord brushed past, made his way to the front of the room.

Everyone shut up, looked up. He claimed the center, paused, grimaced; he was pissed, the basketball coach about to rip into a lazy team.

"I'm not going to waste my time," he said. "Your time, too. What you've heard is true. The young pronghorn antelope was taken last night from the hospital building."

"When?" said Maggie.

"We don't know exactly when, obviously. What we do know is that someone in this room, right now, must be intimately involved in this. Theft," he said, scanned the room. "Let me reassure all of you. We will prosecute this crime to the fullest extent of the law."

"That pronghorn needs expert care," said Maggie. He ignored her.

"I'm talking now to the sick criminal. I know you're here. If you think you know everything about how our security system works, you are tragically mistaken. And just to let you know how seriously we are taking these crimes. There's now a financial reward for knowledge leading to safe return. I want everyone here to know. And the reward is substantial, I promise you. Money talks. If you're a thief, you understand that more than anyone. Know there's a price on your head. That's all you're worth. When you steal from me, no one is your friend."

My mother is a kind of genius of looking. Her masters' thesis, which I once had delivered via Interlibrary loan, was so dense with descriptions and unfamiliar vocabulary I couldn't really read it, though I was also amazed that so much could be written about ten old paintings of mountains and towns and fields and trees.

When I was young, she'd take me to the museum, sit me down on a bench before a canvas by a great master or a student of a great master—a busy Renaissance nativity, angels' heads in circles of rusty gold—and we'd play I Spy, and she'd never tire.

When I was an older child at the museum, and began to complain, she'd send me to the café with ten dollars for a coke and a cookie and after, when I'd returned to where I'd left her, she'd be there, seated, looking.

All the framed paintings on the second floor of our house were originals, landscapes by talented, if regional, artists, modest in content: calm seas, mountain sunset, wheat-field-in-wind. But if I looked closer, even I could see some aspect of the execution that had been handled just right, something beautifully done: the way moonlight had been distributed on the tips of the little waves, a peculiar and perfect strip of bright purple light outlining the face of a cliff, a liquid suggestion of moving shadows.

She has an eye.

But the few paintings downstairs were large vague dramatic smears of color, paintings you might see in Hollywood houses on TV.

She insisted on paying to have the house exterior laboriously cleaned and detailed and repainted every two years. She fired six different lawn care companies during the years I was in high school. She says incredibly unkind things about her own face to herself in the mirror when she thinks no one can hear her.

She told me she wouldn't tell anyone I was spending the summer at the zoo; she said it like she was doing me a favor.

A line in her thesis: "Cezanne painted not to depict the impression of a moment, but to reveal the solid existence undergirding appearances."

After work, the air was thick, the light yellow-green. I biked back to the apartment through an atmosphere unsettled as if from nearby fires. In some directions white clouds had been puffed out and up into cancerous towers; in other directions the clouds were the sleek gray of cruel fish.

The yellow rooms inside the apartment were still and dark, as they always were. I gulped down a glass of water and grabbed an apple, intending to observe the storm from the porch but the window in the bedroom was still open and as I made my way to close it I noticed the way the green dusk outside had poured into the room. I could hear the wind, and the window framed a constellation of shivering trash-tree leaves.

It was like being reminded that I was on a great ship on a journey across an unthinkable ocean. Every window is like an eye and an ear. You can only ever see part of the storm.

I lay down in the center of the floor, to sail through it.

The morning after the storm I got in right on time to the locker room and nearly crashed into a mud-spattered man in a slick, too-large yellow raincoat—Doc—charging out of the bathroom.

"You think you just come in at the usual time?" he said, continued on his way.

"No one told me any different," I said, dumped my bag, followed at his heels.

"What do you think happens here if power goes out? If a tree falls on a fence?"

"I don't know."

"You scared of getting wet?" he said, eyed me.

"No," I said.

"Pick it up, then," he said, and we burst out into the zoo, quick-walked and swooped around the first corner and, as I caught up, I could see down into the rhino enclosure, a sea of orange-red mud, puddles like ponds. The rhinos had been kept inside. There were tree limbs down everywhere, a snowfall of torn off green leaves. At the bottom of the hill, in an otherwise empty grassy enclosure, I could see two raincoats—zookeepers —stomping around. One was on the walkie-talkie. "Goddamn it to hell you couldn't even get a horny dog to fuck your leg," Doc said to the air ahead of him, and he broke into a jog.

Setting off the enclosures in that part of the zoo was a red pipe fence and, between the fence and the interior grass, a concrete drainage-ditch, steep and wide enough to deter adventurers on either side from attempting the breech. Now there was at least a foot of red water in the ditch, floating tree limbs and, I saw, scrambling and sliding back down the side, one of the ostriches, body like a damp head of hair, creepy beak-head like a snake in the process of swallowing a demon, useless wings—reptilian when wet—spread and flailing.

Doc wasn't exactly running, but I was having a hard time keeping up with him. It was clear soon enough that we weren't going around through the normal gate.

"What happened here, Dorothy?" he said, stopping about twenty feet away from the struggling monster. One of the keepers up in the grass of the enclosure, I could see, was holding what looked like a burlap sack in his hand.

"It fell off," he said.

"Sure. It fell off. God damn it. Give it here."

"What, throw it?"

"Yeah throw it," said Doc. The keeper took a few steps and hucked it and it splatted in the water halfway across. He turned back to me. "She's not gonna hurt you bad. You stand your ground and get big and we'll get her back up safe."

"Okay," I said, because that was the only thing I could say. Then Doc was over the fence and on his ass, sliding down into the flooded ditch. He gathered the bag, glanced back up at me.

"What're you waiting for?" he said. I didn't answer but threw my leg over, tried to creep down on the soles of my feet, which slipped right away and I tumbled down on my side, splashing to rest at the bottom of the ditch, instantly soaked through. Doc yanked me up by my shoulder. "Look, you come at her at an angle from the human side, right? You ease her up to me and I'll take her."

"Is there, like, something specific I should do?"

"Look at its head. Think about the size of its brain," he said, crept forward, halfway up the zoo side of the concrete ditch, cat-like. I noticed he was wearing heavy boots and that boots would have been a good idea. I didn't know what to do, so I spread my arms, followed until I was about twenty-feet away, and the ostrich noticed me as its grip failed again and it flopped down on its side. Closer, I spread my arms. "HEY BIRD!" I said. "HEY STUPID!" It smelled terrible, like white shit. It turned away and with a new urgency scrambled against gravity up the slick gray face of the ditch, but this time found one claw of purchase and was up, on the lip of the grass, and there was Doc, hand on its wing, and the bag was over its head, and Doc shook the bird like a father with a wild young son, and the bird struggled, and jerked, and then calmed.

"You didn't tie it off," he said to the keepers. "That's what happens."

"How do I get out?" I said.

Doc peered down at me.

"You gotta find someone to scare you out," he said. "That's the only way it works for sure."

One day after work Caroline wanted a peanut butter shake so I went with her down the road to the Sonic by the movie theater. Her car was a rattling old white Ford, quite clean inside, with a tear in the passenger seat that could only have been made by something very sharp. She turned the radio down before starting the car.

Without asking, she parked in one of the spots without the call box and we got out and sat on one of the picnic tables by the sandbox and playground caged off against the parking lot. The green plastic twisting slide was unusually tall. There was no one playing on the playground. At the far picnic table, a woman dug into a sundae, a baby sleeping in a shaded car seat at her feet.

Caroline ordered the shakes and I sat on top of a picnic table in the shade and Caroline came over and sat on top of the picnic table, too, maybe a little too close, as if by accident, but she didn't move away. Our knees were touching. It was not dramatic. She smelled like suntan lotion and sweat, like a person, not like animals. I noticed again that she had excellent posture.

We talked about our broken bones. She had a broken wrist from jumping off a swing; a broken ankle from jumping out of a tree. "I see a pattern here," I said. I let her feel the hardened nub on the side of a knuckle from the finger I broke catching a basketball stupidly.

We talked about her worries about her upcoming semester of student teaching in Warr Acres on the west side of the city

"It's not the material," she said. "And the teacher's nice enough."

"So what is it?"

"The kids."

"The classrooms are packed in Oklahoma, right? What are there, twenty-five?"

"Thirty," she said. "At least. But it's not that. I mean, it is that. Thirty is way too many. But I'm worried they won't like me."

"They'll love you," I said. "How could they not?"

I heard what I said. She looked at me. We were sitting very close. There was a moment, and I took it. When I kissed her, her mouth was cold and soft and sweet.

After a long moment, she shifted her head down and, slightly, away.

"What was that," she said, looking at an angle toward the ground.

"You tell me," I said.

She smiled. She had a lovely smile, but it was rare.

"I should go," she said.

Living in a city is very different from living on a college campus or living in a suburb. This feeling is strongest late at night. In the suburbs at such times, you step outside and sense the familiar specific darkness on the other side of the fence, in the neighbor's house across the street, blocking you in, keeping you safe. But when you step out of your home in the city in the deep night or even in the dawn, you step into the whole city. If you hear sirens in the distance, there is no sense that they are going somewhere else—if you wait long enough, you will hear them grow louder, and then you will see the flickering lights. There's a cat creeping through the weeds in the unmown lawn next door. There's smoke in the air. You are alone, but you aren't isolated. You want to get on your bike and follow the wind downtown, out to the lake, into the first sunlight. You understand that you live not in your house, but in the world.

I found myself one morning standing in front and slightly to the left of a pregnant llama. In one hand I held a few giant knobby carrots at the ready. The llama gnawed nonchalantly on a mouthful of grass hay.

"What am I supposed to do? What if she bolts?" I said.

"She's a llama," said Maggie, "not a wolverine. And Marcy's a sweet old girl besides. Just stand there and offer her carrots and don't make sudden moves."

We were in the concrete-floored stall behind the enclosure. Maggie had a roll-up sonogram machine that looked to me like a very old computer connected to beige alien probes on wires. She splorped pale blue goo from a ketchup bottle on one of the probes. I showed the llama one of the longest carrots and she opened her lips to accept it. The llama didn't react when Maggie pressed the probe, gently, into her belly.

"See," said Maggie. "Mama llama don't care."

"Mama llama don't like drama," I said. Maggie didn't respond. She was absorbed in her work, turning behind her as she moved the probe carefully across the llama's belly to see where she was on a flickering monitor. "You could move the screen closer to you."

"Machines spook mothers sometimes," she said.

I turned my attention to the carrot eater. Up close, its neck seemed stronger and firmer, like one big muscle. Its teeth were yellow and too large, but other than that not un-human. Its ears, perked up, were surprisingly deep. Its nostrils were uneven. It was not concerned or unconcerned with my presence; she accepted me.

"What do you think is going on with the animals getting stolen?" I said.

"I don't want to think about it," Maggie said and continued with her work.

"I mean, what do you do with a bunch of random weird animals anyway when you can just go to the zoo?"

"They're probably selling them," said Maggie, sharply, and maybe pressed the probe a little too hard. The llama paused mid-chew. Maggie pulled the probe off, turned for more blue goo. "You can get a lot of money for these animals if you know who to talk to. There are lots of small animal parks who don't follow the rules. Private collections. People call some animals 'exotics.' Some people just want to. Keep them." She had to pause. She collected herself. "Like trophies in tiny cages. What kind of life is that."

"I didn't know," I said. "I thought there was only, like, real zoos."

"You learn quick how terrible the world can be, working here," she said. She placed one open hand against the llama's ribs. "But not today, right mama? Not today."

"Who cares about what people want? What do they know about anything?" said Doc. We were pitchforking grass hay into the hoofstock enclosures.

"Isn't that what a zoo is for? So people can see?"

"If you look at it the stupid way. The fundamental mission of a zoo is zoological preservation and protection; visitors just pay the bills."

"I guess," I said.

"No, not 'I guess.' This is important. What do people want to see at the zoo?"

"Animals."

"Which ones?"

"Big ones," I said.

"You see any cows here?"

"Big animals you don't see every day."

"Like what?"

"Lions and tigers. Polar bears. Pandas."

"Pandas! Right, pandas. We should care about people who think pandas are worth looking at. Fucking pandas, panda fucking cameras on all day. Pandas."

"What's wrong with pandas?"

"What's wrong with pandas? You know what a panda eats, right? Bamboo. Worst fucking diet on earth. No nutrition. You may as well eat a stack of PVC pipe. And they're so enormous they need to eat a whole fucking forest every day. They can only get pregnant a couple days a year and they are so bad at screwing they end up injuring each other and so stupid half the time when the cub is born they squish it. Only animal that belongs on God's green earth less is a human being."

61

"So you don't like pandas."

"Wiseass. And use your shoulders, not your back."

"I don't know why," I said, swallowed. "I guess you could say I'm on a search. I want to figure out how to live."

Caroline grinned, I could tell, though it was too dark to see all of her. We were leaning on opposite posts of my front steps; it was very late, hot, still.

"What?" I said.

"Nothing," she said. "That's cool. I mean, I understand."

"Then what's funny?"

"It's just. Using a summer to go on a search. Like some king told you to go on a quest. I mean. It's hard enough to get through a day. My friend's textbooks for her nursing classes this summer cost four-hundred dollars."

"When I was coming up in Kansas City," said Maggie, "there was a keeper there, a very respected older woman, who did a lot of her work with the kangaroos. A good keeper. One night there's a big storm, just like that one we had in June, and one of the nursing mother kangaroos freaks out and abandons her baby. Now once that's done, it's done, you see? She's a kangaroo. She's who she is. When the baby's out of sight, the cord is cut. And the roo, she's too young to be out of the pouch. She's like a preemie, really, that needs a month in an incubator. And no one knows what to do. They try to introduce her back to her mother and that doesn't work. The head keeper has this idea about heating up a plastic box. And then this one keeper, this older woman, decides to invent this sort of substitute pouch. It's just a big purse with a bunch of sterile gauze wrapped around inside it. But no one knows what to do so they all get together to decide fine, do it, and she carries that little roo in her purse around all day. Bottle feeds her, just like you would. Takes her home with her because it wasn't safe to leave her alone. Just like a human baby."

"So what happened?" I said. "She steal it?"

"No, she didn't steal her. You think that's why I was talking about this? If you love an animal, you don't steal it. That's selfish."

"Okay."

"She cared for her. That's the point of the story. That's the job. She carried that kangaroo around night and day, kept her warm and well fed, until she was old enough to go back into population. And she did. She still followed the keeper around whenever she visited. But she grew up. Became who she was supposed to be. And she's still alive, as far as I know. You could go see her today."

"So what's your game?" said Doc. I was roughly chopping one billion carrots.

"Sorry?"

"Your plan. Why you're here."

"It's a good internship."

"That's it?"

"That's it."

"You don't know what you're doing around basic lab equipment. You don't go on and on about how much you love baby elephants. You one of those psychological animal behavior types?"

"Maybe."

"I once knew a man, smart man, well-published scientist, spent five summers in a box in a tree staring at geese. That sound interesting to you?" I tried to imagine it. The same box, day after day. The loud quiet of the woods and the lake. The smell of damp plywood. The million stupid black and white birds always in my vision, in the binoculars; my eyes always in the lake dozens of feet away from my body. I see the geese in the whole frame, filling up my whole eyes. Only geese.

"Maybe."

"Maybe means no," said Doc.

"You're right," I said.

"So why are you here?" he said.

"One thing led to another," I said.

"That's your reason, huh?" he said. I thought for a moment he was going to pound me on the shoulder in a manly way, but he clapped his gloved hands together, satisfied, and continued on his way. "Sounds like an excuse to me."

Watching people at the zoo from inside an animal enclosure is both dreamlike and clarifying, like looking at something across the room through binoculars.

It is especially easy to observe the true strangeness of people at the zoo because they are looking for somewhere to rest their attention that is not you, so their eyes slide off you, like you aren't even there.

Certain hefty men in T-shirts tight over their bellies have to walk as if their bellies are held out, as an offering, to the world they are walking into.

Children in radioactive neon T-shirts look deeply and quickly, with desperation; when they spot an animal it's as obvious as if someone stuck a pin into their thumb.

If you watch teenagers carefully, you can see that they often, but not always, are only pretending to not care about the rest of the world.

Part of my morning routine became checking on specific areas of grass inside enclosures that sometimes needed to be watered by hand because the sprinklers had to be turned off by the time the walkways flooded with gawkers. At first I was afraid. The first time, on the walk out to the zoo with the list in my hand, the new walkie-talkie squawking on my belt, I asked Maggie: "Do tortoises bite?"

"Only if they catch you," she said. "And you're a blade of grass."

"What if they smell something weird on me?"

"Titan's got a fiber boot on and he's eighty-five."

"Right."

"You'll get used to it," she said.

It's true and sad that entering sealed-off space inhabited by wild animals became less and less strange. Soon enough I was staring at the muck and white flamingo shit I was spraying off the rock with the hose, not the flamingo an arm's length away who was sleeping on one foot, neck folded and twisted so she could rest her own beaky head on the pillow of her own pink back. But I never lost that little gulp of wonder in the mornings with the tortoises. Frequently they'd gotten wet in the sprinkler so they were shiny; they were like rocks with souls pressing their faces into the grass; they moved like gleaming statues coming to life.

I got into the habit of texting Caroline an emoji of whatever animal I was just about to attend to, if there was such an emoji: snake, elephant, giraffe. She'd reply with faces making inappropriate emotions: embarrassment, wild excitement, tears.

Some mornings I'd wake to find she'd sent me a beast impossible to encounter in life: blue whale, dinosaur, unicorn.

We often went for peanut butter shakes after work; she refused to let me pay.

Because of the of the nature of the internship—its value to ambitious academic zoology types—we were required to meet every Friday afternoon for group discussions, for collection of the required weekly "tasklist spreadsheet" and "analytical reflection." I am sure I was the only intern who regularly had to bike feverishly to the nearest branch library during lunch break on Friday to finish and print them. I more than once turned them in wet with the sweat of my hands.

The discussions themselves were much more tangible and focused than discussions in college. We had a variety of keepers visit to talk at length about a topic of personal interest, such as the logistical tangles that arose when caring for, and encouraging the reproduction of, a species of endangered horned lizards. I listened hard and felt myself learning, like watching a train lay its own track as it moved. After the presentation, one of the other interns jumped in with some eager comments about his undergraduate research on the specific nutritional value of particular insects for different reptile species. His pants were tucked into his laced-up still-new-looking work boots.

At one point, he said, "Of course, we can't all be ovoviviparous," and half the room laughed. Especially one of the keepers, who laughed like a choking stork, but in a charming way.

I did enjoy listening, but I didn't feel like one of them most of the time, and especially when they started talking like the scientists they were. I came to understand that not only did they share a vocabulary, but, in their laughter and attention, they also shared a deep understanding that their studies and work were not only interesting but worthwhile, meaningful, a true life.

At the same time, I knew how rarely zoo visitors spent any time at all observing those rare lizards in their extremely well-maintained environment because, for one thing, the lizards preferred to spend their days buried in sand.

Some mornings—not every morning—I would wake up and feel wrong, nervous, dizzy, tipped backwards, like I'd fallen asleep on a playground slide.

I had to breathe and tell myself that the surface of the world was effectively flat, that gravity worked, that nothing terrible was going to happen.

I had to stand up, slowly, like an old man, and look at my own face in the blank bathroom's mirror and tell myself it was a face.

What is your problem, really? I'd ask myself.

I'd shake my head to try to shake the feeling away and I'd hear the silence of the yellow apartment that was not mine, wish there was another voice somewhere, a name to speak.

I think it was good there was no one to talk to, no way to get rid of the feeling.

The bike ride to work settled me, the way a tire is always in contact with the road, the way you can make your own wind by moving against air.

On the bike rides to work, first on smooth streets past churches and bungalows and neatly kept small homes with white SUVs in the short driveways, I often found myself remembering one article I'd come across while working on an essay for my Introduction to International Studies seminar, a final Gen-Ed requirement I'd been putting off and only signed up for because it was a Thursday evening class I planned to B-minus my way through. I don't remember what the actual essay I wrote ended up being about. The article was about the experience of refugees fleeing Vietnam during the war. It was unlike me to read such articles as opposed to scanning them in order to cherry pick a quote or two. I must have been tired or over-caffeinated or high or all three. There was a story of a mother having walked to the sea over mountains carrying her child, a girl, two or three years old. This was a story from a witness, someone who was on the boat with her. The child was feverish when they got on the boat. There was no medicine and very little fresh water. At some point during the second night, the child died. There were not many details in this story, nothing about how dark it was, what the sea smelled like, what they heard and felt. But the truth was that the woman held the child, felt her own child grow cold, grow stiff. In the morning everyone knew the child had to be thrown overboard. There was the question of disease. There was not enough room for everyone on the boat as it was. They tried to take the child from her but the woman would not let her go. She stood and held her dead child and turned and leapt into the sea and was gone.

I was helping Maggie and another intern up on ladders install a new wooden climbing apparatus—what they called an enrichment—in the spider monkey cage. We had to pull down an older, splitting and damp-looking hanging lattice, and we found that somehow there was a yellow mushy banana jammed up high in the corner, between a hunk of wood and the mesh netting.

"I wish we had been on a behavioral study," said the intern. "What could this mean?"

"It means at least one of those monkeys must be hungry," said Maggie, more sad than worried.

It turned out one of the other interns—the one with a backpack festooned with patches with names of what seemed to be big rocks—had the previous morning climbed up there and jammed in a banana in the corner to "give the monkeys a little challenge!" Everyone thought this was very funny, except Maggie, who was mostly relieved.

"I held Harry when he was two days old," she said to me the next morning.

"Okay," I said.

"The hungry spider monkey," she said.

"Of course. Right," I said.

"His sister, Sherry. She was taken." I didn't know what to say. "When a monkey is a baby," she said, "it's just a little bit less helpless than a person."

I tried to imagine it, but could not.

"I haven't even held a real baby since, I don't know," I said. "Maybe my cousin? At a wedding like six years ago?"

I remembered thinking, this is heavy.

This is a small idea, but I believe it firmly: I think the Big Cat Forest enclosures should be rearranged so you are forced to encounter the leopards in this order: Forest, Clouded, Snow.

Caroline didn't invite me to the party she was having at her house directly but she talked about it as if I was going. "Maybe you'll even meet my first boyfriend," she said. "When we were together, he was trying to become a famous skateboarder on YouTube."

Her parents were going on a marriage retreat with their church somewhere in the Arbuckle mountains. I couldn't imagine my parents doing any such thing.

"What happens? Do they just sit by the campfire and pray?"

"If it's anything like vacation bible camp," said Caroline and, then, thoughtfully, "I think they're going to get out of the city and away from us and everything for a few days."

"That's harsh," I said.

"Not really," she said.

"Didn't they tell you not to have a party?" I said.

"Of course they did," she said. "But it's not, like, a party party."

She asked if I thought it was too far to ride on my bike, and I was thinking that maybe it was too far to ride on my bike, so I knew I had to ride there on my bike.

It was a storm-free evening. I set out before and then through dusk, the heat as usual refusing to evaporate. It seemed like there should have been a breeze, but there was not. It was an annoying ride, but not because it was hard; it was flat and unlovely. I had to pick my way through anxious mall traffic, then zoom through a golf course and a stretch of big houses even newer and uglier than in the gated community where I grew up, trucks with lawn care trailers everywhere, the insect-screaming of a million weed-whackers scratching up the last of the daylight.

When I finally emerged into her neighborhood, it was dark enough that I had to turn on the bike's blinking lights that were robot-bumblebee ridiculous.

The houses were brick ranches: small front porches crowded with mostly well-tended potted plants and chairs, a few people on their porches, a garage open and lit up with a few people sitting inside on lawn chairs, a whiff of pot, no sidewalks. Even the smallest houses had several cars jammed in the driveway, parked on the street. So different from my childhood neighborhood of houses with cavernous garages set separately from each other and no one ever outside.

When the numbers started getting close, I flicked off the lights.

Her parents' house was a neat brick ranch not different from the rest of the neighborhood. There were cars in the driveway, on the street, but not out of proportion to the surrounding houses. There was music on inside the house, but not louder than maybe an old man with bad hearing watching a war movie turned way up so he could actually hear it.

I was surprised to see a red For Sale By Owner sign pressed into the square of front lawn—Caroline had never mentioned it.

I straddled my bike looking at the ordinary yellow light in the windows, trying to figure out what rapping country song was being played for a minute, before I recognized that there was someone sitting on the front step, still as a shadow. The porch light was either burned out or turned off.

Whoever it was, they'd been watching me for as long as I had been watching the house.

I dismounted and pushed my bike up the driveway and rested it against the garage.

The shadow on the steps didn't react. It was a young man, so tall he had to sort of hunch, lean forward, knees pointing out like wings, to sit on the steps. He was wearing a white Thunder jersey that hung off the wire-hanger of his shoulders; his arms were too thin; I thought of the legs of storks. It was Caroline's brother.

"Hey," I said. He nodded without looking up. As I got closer I could smell the grassy sweetness of pot rising from him and could see his eyes sticky and half-closed in the dim light leaking from the windows. He was well and truly baked. Someone thumped on the front door from the inside. I sat down next to him on the other side of the steps.

"I'm Zack," I said, "from the zoo."

"That sounds like a cartoon character," he said. "Zoo Zack."

"I guess you're right."

"Zoo Zack from the moon," he said. "I remember."

"Why're you out here?" I said.

"No reason," he said. "Fresh air." The air was thick as greasy steam. I was swimming in my own sweat.

"Caroline inside?" I said.

"Do you love her?" he said.

"What?"

"I asked if you loved her."

"That seems like a lot to ask, out of the blue."

"It's just a question." We sat there together. The song changed; someone inside hollered: "You're seriously *crazy*."

"Are you guys close?" I said.

"Shouldn't you know?"

"I don't know," I said. "I only met her a few weeks ago."

"That's a long time," he said.

"She told me you'd been sick," I said and wished I hadn't right away.

He didn't seem to mind. He smiled.

"Not right now," he said.

"I should go in," I said.

"You be good to her," he said, tipped his face up to me. His face floated in the dark; he looked like he was trying to open his eyes as wide as he could, to see me, to let me know he was looking at me. It was sort of touching, sort of a threat, and funny because of how high he was. He was so young, a kid. But no one had ever looked at me like that before. I touched his shoulder on my way up the stairs before I saw it was something an uncle would do.

On the abbreviated porch there were two dining table chairs, an upside-down Frisbee full of probably water, a row of cacti in pots, a red cup half full of beer and cigarette butts.

I opened the door without bothering to knock.

At first I wondered, stupidly, if I was at the wrong house. The song insisted over and over "girl get up in my truck" to what seemed at first like an empty room. On one wall was a long mirror and a cross made of pewter, curlicued inside a frame. Opposite that was a wall full of family photographs, and in one, there was Caroline, much younger, smiling publicly in a way she did not smile, showing her teeth.

Beneath the photos, four people were playing Scrabble on the carpet, between an overstuffed easy chair and a long overstuffed beige couch. They were maybe my age and maybe halfway through the game. They'd pushed a glass coffee table into the wall to make room. One boy was sitting Indian style and resting his chin on his clasped hands. I could sense that none of them had had even a sip of beer. One cradled an unopened bottle of iced tea. They did not look up to see who had walked in.

To my right there was a little room with paned-glass doors, a flickering in the darkness and a rumbling thump that was different from the music—a TV room, lumpy shadows playing video games, creating familiar beautiful explosions.

The music was coming from a different doorway, one that led into kitchen brightness. Beyond the brightness, there were distant voices, hooting—in the backyard, most likely, the usual nonsense going on out there.

When I stepped into the kitchen, Caroline was leaning against the sink. The refrigerator was wide open, and on the counter were two full handles of rum and a torn-open 30-pack. Her friend Kaylee in the corner looked over, chewing on her lip; they'd been talking about something serious. Kaylee was wearing short-shorts and an abbreviated white halter-top with little purple flowers on the straps, her eyes lined in silver glitter; she'd dressed up. Caroline was wearing the same thing she'd worn to the movies—T-shirt and cut-offs. Her feet were bare. She was flushed, like she'd just come back from a run. But in the wet intensity of her eyes and the set of her mouth, I could tell she was lit with anger.

"She's not mad at you," said Kaylee to me.

"Don't tell him that," said Caroline. She closed her eyes, tipped her head back, as if to drink the rain.

"What's going on?" I said.

"Nothing," she said.

"He didn't mean anything by it," Kaylee told Caroline, wrapping up the private talk I'd walked in on. "It's just something people say."

"What's something people say?" I said.

"*'It's all part of God's plan,'*" said Caroline.

"I had a friend who would say that after Cowboys games," I said.

"I'm not joking," said Caroline.

"Clearly," I said.

Then Kaylee stepped forward, closed the refrigerator door and came to me, clasping my forearm with two hands. Her fingers were thin and smooth.

"Come on," she said. "I'll introduce you to some people. Give her a minute."

The backyard was small but neatly kept. Sparse but mown grass, crepe myrtles along the back fence. Gas grill and patio furniture. Her friends out back were the drinkers—there was a game of asshole going on around a glass table, a couple kids standing around smoking, one floppy-haired doofus trying to show off his inability to juggle a soccer ball. It was more like a high school party than what I had gotten used to in college. People were friendly, asked me about what it was like taking care of giraffes and lions (I couldn't help but think of Doc saying, out of the side of his mouth, "Fucking charismatic megafauna."). I told the story of chasing the ostrich up out of the puddled ditch. I kept my eye on the back door, but Caroline didn't come out.

After two beers, I caught up with Kaylee grinding out the spark of a cigarette with the sole of her sandal, then bending over to pick it up so she could throw it away. No one ever did that at parties I went to.

"She ever going to come out?" I said.

"Probably. It's her brother."

I glanced around the backyard, but he was nowhere, maybe still sitting on the front steps, alone.

"She's mad at her brother?" I said.

"Dude. He almost died, and he's getting sick again."

"I thought he was getting better," I said.

"Dude," she said.

Caroline came out about half an hour later. The sky was blank hot dark. I was talking to Kaylee about skiing (she'd never been) when she appeared next to me. She slid her arm around my back like we'd been a couple for years.

"What was all that in the kitchen?" I said.

"Nothing," she said.

"Why are your parents selling their house?"

"It's dark now," she said, as if that answered anything. But then she rested her cheekbone against the point of my shoulder, bone to bone, in a way no one ever had. It was like something an animal would do; something inside me unlocked. I was glad to have her next to me. "Can we not talk about it?" she said.

"Sure," I said. "I'm here."

I was on my way out to check on the grass and greet my morning tortoises when Maggie caught me by the elbow. She looked like she was about to tell me my dog had died.

"Doctor Colcord wants to see you," she said.

"What does that mean?" I said.

"I don't know," she said.

His office was down the administrative hallway I'd never had to go down. That hallway was not exactly like a "real office"—not like the few times I'd visited my father at work, with the linen-white walls, the buzzing silence, the men in sharply creased suits and the women in restrictive skirts taking small quick steps. Many of the doors on the zoo hall were open; there was music— Rolling Stones?—from one of the open doors. Vivid framed photographs of animals on the walls—a peacock in full display, the length of a bright green dangling viper, mother/child elephants in embrace. It was friendly; it smelled like sprayed flowery air freshener.

Dr. Colcord's door was the only one in the hall that was closed. Through the frosted glass I could see that the light was on, so I knocked.

"Wait," came the word. So I waited. One minute later the door swung open and there was Dr. Colcord, blinking, like he'd just come out of a pool.

His office was not what I'd imagined; I'd expected some kind of cheesy lacquer-shiny black desk, gold paperweights. It was messy. There were two crammed full bookshelves against one wall. A desk covered with papers, a desktop computer, an open laptop. One wall was large windows looking out toward the zoo, though you couldn't see much more than trees and one near corner of the hoofstock enclosure: the actual animals, I knew by now, mainly congregated by the ditches and puddles further in. Above the computers, there was another shelf full of what could have been things from a museum: carved masks, fossilized fish bones, what looked like a wrought iron cage for hummingbirds.

"Have a seat," he said, not unfriendly at all, directing me to an elegant furniture-catalog black chair.

"Thanks," I said, and did as I was told.

"Well," he said, settling himself into a spaceship chair behind the desk, "Zachary. You're probably wondering why I asked you here today."

"Yeah," I said.

"I'll keep this brief. Your application stuck out; I thought so when it first came across my desk months ago." He smiled. I couldn't read him at all. "I realized why—your name is familiar. I know your father. More by reputation than experience, though, to be fair. I spent some time in development at the Dallas Zoo. We moved in similar circles."

"Everyone knows my father," I said. It came out more sullenly than I intended; I'd meant to simply state a fact.

"It's a great advantage," he said. "To come from excellence."

"Absolutely," I said, nodding vigorously, to make up for whatever ungratefulness I'd implied.

"You don't have a typical background for this internship. What you do have is the coursework that suggest you've been thinking about law school, following in your father's footsteps. Is that still in your mind?"

"Yes, sir," I said, quickly, and could not stop myself from going on. "The summer here and then I'm going to take a year as a research assistant to learn about the lay of the land." He nodded. "Maybe travel a bit," I couldn't help adding, because it felt like something a person in my position would say.

"I think it's smart," he said, "a summer here and then a year in the trenches. Shows wide-ranging interests, outside-of-the-box thinking. And I hear good things from your supervisors, which speaks well of your flexibility and work ethic."

"Thank you," I said.

"Thank *you*," he said. "So I just want you to know, in the future, if you need a reference. I would be happy to do what I can, given your record. Here in Oklahoma City, people know each other's names, people know my name, and there's nothing more important than your name. I'm sure your father would tell you the same."

"Absolutely," I said automatically.

"That's one reason why animals disappearing worries me so much, especially at a time when many of our energy-industry-aligned donors have to make difficult strategic decisions. I'm sure your father is familiar with the circumstances, the markets." He put one hand face down on a stack of papers. "Have you heard the phrase herding cats?" he said.

"I have," I said.

"The task of my position is sometimes more like herding jellyfish," he said, smiled, pleased with himself. I imagined it. A floating mob of them, purple, glowing. "So I can count on you?" he said. "You'll look out for us?"

"Of course," I said, before I understood that he was asking me to do something and I had agreed.

"Good. Well, I don't want to keep you from your work. Let's talk again. I've myself been in your shoes. I know how helpful it can be to be offered a hand up."

There was a moment early one morning when I was with Maggie in the empty brown-bear enclosure with the flat thin silver shovel and the rake, shuffling through the sprinkler-wet grass on the look-out for what she called scat when my mind was blank and I saw my mind was blank and I stopped and looked up and looked behind me and could not remember taking the steps I'd just taken. I'd been at the zoo a handful of weeks and already I'd slipped back into nowhere.

Everyone gets bored and tired, I told myself. Just because you get bored and tired and stupid once doesn't mean the world disappears.

The artificial but convincingly churning little river along the enclosure whispered and sparkled brownly. I could see from where I stood on the opposite side of the walkway the giant plaque of a bald eagle with outspread wings. A bald eagle's wingspan can be as wide as 7 feet; they have a pouch in their throats in which they store for later regurgitation the indigestible bones of small mammals such as mice and rabbits.

I was on my way to the herps with Doc for reasons I hadn't asked about when there was a man in a fitted black T-shirt, sunglasses on the back of his head, boy toddler trailing, stomping down the path past the condor cage hollering "Bella! Bella!" Lost children were not unusual; the apparent danger was not serious. There's no easy way to disappear from the zoo (a fact which made, to me, the story of the missing animals more mysterious than troubling).

There was only one way in and out for normal human visitors, even lost children, plus there was an army of zoo-polo'd staff with walkie-talkies listening for word of a lost child who was never as lost as the parent was.

Doc stopped the hollering man. Said "Wait." Said, without concern, "how old, hair color, what the kid is wearing." He listened and without looking said, "there." He pointed over the man's shoulders to the flamingos, and there was a little girl in a green Tinkerbell dress with her fingers in her mouth, chest against the fence, absorbed.

"Bella!" barked the man as if he hadn't seen her, and he took off for her, his toddler son again following well behind.

Doc continued on as if nothing had happened.

"How'd you know?" I said.

"It's like anything else. Pattern recognition," said Doc. "You have instincts if you know how to let them work."

An hour later we were in a damp room full of blue light separating out a bale of local turtles for transport to a state park exhibit when another not-all-that-rare squawking call came across the walkie-talkie:

"Seven-year old boy, OU Football T-shirt, blond hair, Nicholas answers to Nicky. Last seen on the carousel-side playground. Repeat: carousel-side playground."

That playground was not far from where we were.

"Kid's looking at the red pandas," said Doc, slapping an open gloved hand on a water-drenched counter.

"You gonna call something in?"

But he was already peeling off his gloves, stomping out. I lidded the turtle tank, followed.

Right away I saw the mother—giant floppy lavender gardener's hat against the sun—in tears, circling the condor exhibit on the way to the carousel. She was peering wildly about, into the cage where the condor perched asleep, as if that gawky ancient bird had stolen the child. A visitors' services person trailed behind, failing to get her attention.

Doc blew past. He didn't stop at the carousel, or even the nightmare-candy-colored playground, but made directly for the red panda enclosure.

It was a small exhibit—there were only two red pandas, and they weren't particularly active, especially in the heat of the day—but there was a significant pack of gawkers, pressing forward, because the red pandas were, in Doc's words, "cute little assholes."

I could tell by the way Doc halted, well away from the exhibit, backs of wrists on his hips, that he had not spotted the boy as he'd expected.

I caught up.

"He's not here?" I said, as non-confrontationally as I could. I was surprised he didn't instantly snap at me.

"When I'm wrong about an animal," he said, (a

child, I thought), "it's usually because of a human."

While he chewed on his lip, I looked down the path, into the crowd and saw, not far away, a seven-year old blond boy in a maroon OU Football T-shirt riding gleefully atop the shoulders of a bounding teenage boy with the same blond hair. A brother. The boy had spotted his brother and run off. Simple enough.

Then Doc was looking where I was looking. He unbuttoned the chest pocket of his shirt and removed from it, to my astonishment, one bright green cellophane-wrapped lollipop. He passed it to me.

"Won't need this now," he said. "But you may want to give it to him, if the mother gets angry and he starts to cry."

He turned to retreat to the room of the blue light and the turtles, leaving me to oversee the reunion of mother and sons.

On Sundays some people came directly from brunch after church: the little girls in dresses in floral print dresses, the fathers in pleated khakis and tucked-in polos in Easter-y shades, the families walking more closely together than other families. They had the cleanliness of a catalog or a political ad; there was something false about them.

I asked Caroline. She was on her break, granola bar and Dr. Pepper at the picnic table near the train station that got mist from the mister if the breeze was strong enough.

"You don't go to church, for one thing," she said. "So you have one idea of what people who go there are like and you just see your own idea whenever you look at them."

"My mom still goes sometimes."

"Right. Sometimes."

"What do you think then? If you know better than me."

"You can't generalize about church people," she said. "There's all kinds."

"So you think it's not just a show? They're really like that?"

"Of course it's a show," she said. "Just not how you think it is. They aren't that way because they're showing off. They're that way because they're scared."

"Scared of what?"

"You figure it out."

I didn't spend much time actively worrying about the vanished animals. And there had been a lot of them, according to Maggie: a few pronghorns, a few lemurs, a few storks, the one spider monkey and another quite old and frail spider monkey who had been removed from public view, some newborn turtles, a pair of mesa foxes, some not really rare Muscovy ducks (though it was also possible the ducks had merely escaped). I hadn't been attached to the zoo for long enough to feel her sense of loss.

Even after the odd conversation with Dr. Colcord, I was avoiding thinking about the future. It was more important to me to imagine as deeply as possible what it would feel like to have antlers.

When we were all given a bright pink piece of paper that informed us they had hired additional security guards, I assumed that would be the end of it.

A week later a sandhill crane was gone.

There are some dumpsters by the hospital building. I didn't think anything of them. Everywhere humans exist, there are dumpsters. I went out of the side door of the hospital once at Maggie's direction with a bag stuffed full of what smelled like rotting hay and bleach and could hear the rumble of an idling garbage truck—not unusual, since the hospital building was right off of an access road where food delivery came in and out. What was unusual was to see Doc, stomping back toward me. As soon as he spotted me, he started tugging off baby-blue latex gloves.

"Hurry up now, kid," he said.

"I'm trying," I said. The bag was getting heavier, and I was occupied with it until I turned the corner and saw, not the truck angling its prongs into one of the dumpsters, or lifting a dumpster to fling its contents into its own opened back, or pulling away, but a man next to the truck, thin and green-jumpsuited, facing away from me toward the empty far corner of the elephant enclosure, smoking a cigarette. I managed to fling the bag neatly enough up into the nearest open dumpster, and the man started to say something, something like, "You always want," as he turned, and saw me and froze. His face was deeply lined, but his hair was thick and black.

"Who are you?" he said.

"I work here," I said. I didn't see how strange the moment was until I was halfway back to the hospital: Doc didn't just have a friend, which was surprising in itself—he had a friend who drove a garbage truck into and out of the zoo.

The first week of August, Caroline and I both had Wednesday off. Wondering if we'd have another free day together before the summer was over was the first time the idea of the summer ending attempted to enter my consciousness. She said she'd pick me up in the morning which meant, not totally to my surprise, exactly 7:30.

I was sitting on the front step putting on my shoes when she pulled up. I'd been trying to wear shoes as little as possible.

She was wearing running shorts and a plain black one-piece swimsuit that looked like it was from a swim team. I hadn't ever seen her shoulders; they were freckled, paler than the summer suggested they should be. She wasn't the sort to lay in the sun.

"Do I need a swim suit?" I said.

"You'll dry," she said, pulling away.

We drove south for a certain amount of time, into what I'd always thought of as the nowhere between Oklahoma City and Dallas. Oceans of tall grass, billboards for casinos. I tried to look harder, to not let it blur by, but it was difficult. Maybe the better way to understand a vastness is not with your eyes. It was already hot enough that the air from open windows was like being blasted with loud clean sunshine.

When we turned off the highway Caroline asked me what I was thinking about and I said "sunlight."

I asked her what she was thinking about and she said, "I'm driving."

She drove us to the national park in Sulfur. We drove in on a dirt road through thick woods alongside a rushing brook, little campsites on either side, sturdy tents, picnic tables, bright plastic coolers. The parking lot was mostly full; there was a wide pool in a bend in the stream and a little falls. A dozen kids in the water, a couple with elaborate assault-rifle-sized neon-green waterguns. A few chubby T-shirted teenage boys taking turns leaping in. A packed trash can buzzing with flies. I could imagine my mother's face; she wouldn't even go into the immaculate country club pool except for adult swim, even when I was just learning and was afraid of putting my eyes underwater.

We got out. I made my way toward the water and Caroline tugged lightly on the sleeve of my T-shirt, guiding me away from the swimming hole past the ranger station, taking a packed-gravel path into the woods. Soon the world was cooler, speckled with light and shadow, humming. She held my hand; an old couple with cameras, the woman carrying a long gray feather, passed by. They smiled at us like they knew something about us.

Caroline pulled us off of the gravel path onto a barely visible track of pounded dirt, flowering on all sides with poison ivy; I had to let go of her hand and walk carefully.

"Are you taking me somewhere to murder me?" I said.

"Think of this as the next challenge on your quest," she said.

"Ha ha," I said.

It was not long before we could hear water, and the path ended by spreading out into the bank of a smaller stream, some kind of tributary, a steady rushing edged with mud. There was long flat rock in a corner of the stream, large enough to stretch out on. Caroline stomped there across the water, clambered up and settled in, wrapped her arms around her knees and pressed her face to her knees and looked down into the water. I wondered if she was crying. The woods were electric with insects I couldn't see.

I made my way to the stone and joined her.

"What's up?" I said.

"You see the snake?" she said.

"Fuck," I said. "No," and whipped my head around, and there it was, at least two feet long, black patterned monster, lazily coiled around itself like a bit of tossed extension cord, on the bank just beyond the long flat rock.

Snakes are invisible until you see them; then, they are all you see.

"You could have warned me," I said.

"I would have," she said. "I wanted to give you a chance."

"Should I throw a rock at it or something?"

"Let it be," she said. "You're around snakes all the time."

"Not free," I said.

"Now you are."

"What is this place?" I said. "Have you come here before?"

"It's quiet," she said. I peeled her hands away from her knees and she looked at me. She looked like she was about to say she was fine.

"You want to talk?" I said.

"About what?"

"I don't know," I said. "Your brother."

"What point is there in talking about anything?" she said. "It's all in God's hands now. That's what everyone says so it must be the truth."

"It's that bad?"

"It's going to get worse."

"It's okay to be sad about it," I said, and she leaned into me. I had to throw my hand down to hold myself up. She was practically on top of me, one hand pressing into my stomach, kissing me with her fierce soft mouth, eyes closed.

"Hey," I muffled. Her eyes snapped open; she bit my lip, pulled back.

"What?" she said.

"I don't know. You seem upset."

"Yeah?" she said, slid a finger just inside the waistband of my shorts, let her palm rest, gently, just there. "You think so?" she said. "What?"

She kissed hard. It was good, uncomfortable. Every so often I checked on the snake, who didn't move.

"You can talk to me," I said after. "You can say whatever you want to say." I was lying on my back on the warm shadowed rock, without my shirt—Caroline had thrown it in the water and now it was spread out and drying. Caroline was sitting next to me, finishing the last of the joint she'd brought, cheap but effective weed, well-rolled.

"I know," she said.

"I mean, I care about you. I know I'm leaving and you're going back to school. But I'm being honest."

"I feel that," she said, flicked the burnt roach into the water. "It's just, what is there to say? I went my whole life knowing I was going to heaven, and everyone I love would be there. And now I know that's not true. I know it deep down in me. I know it. And my brother thinks he's going to heaven. And my mother does, and my father does. And he's going to die. It's simple. It's completely simple."

"I don't know what to say," I said.

"No," she said. I pulled myself up, to hold her; she let me, as still and warm as the rock we were sitting on. I looked for the snake but it was gone. I knew it was somewhere nearby, under some stone, burrowed in some hole. I couldn't see the snake but it was real.

For whatever reason, during a frustrating afternoon struggling with the netting around the fisher cat enclosure, I was reminded of a passage from a textbook on modern philosophy. After too much phone-Googling, I found it again. It was a supposition about how an animal learns, written by an excellently named French philosopher, Maurice Merleau-Ponty: "Because it proceeds unsteadily, by trial and error, and has at best a meager capacity to accumulate knowledge, it displays very clearly the struggle involved in existing in a world into which it has been thrown, a world to which it has no key."

I texted the passage to myself and read it to Maggie the next morning when she was checking out her walkie-talkie.

"Are you trying to bum me out?" she said.

And then there was Doc, just barely in the hall, waiting for Maggie to finish so he could sign-out his own walkie-talkie.

"Kid," he said, "you are way over your skis."

Later I read it to Caroline. She said, "Duh."

"What do you think happens," said Doc one afternoon inside the giraffe enclosure, "when one of these beasts dies?"

"I don't know," I said. "Do the other ones start wailing or something?"

"I'm not talking about behavior," he said. "I'm talking biological mass. Weight. What happens to the body?"

"You bury it?"

"With what? A giant backhoe? In what garage do we house this backhoe? And where would we dig the hole? And how would we get the giraffe into the hole in the first place?"

"I don't know. Throw it in the river. You tell me."

"Don't give up. That's lazy. Think about it. What else could you do with a dead body?"

"You could cremate it, right?"

"You could. It's a body. It's flesh and bone. If you can burn up a person you could burn up a giraffe. What are the complications?"

"Complications?"

"Can you just set a match to a dead giraffe and walk away?"

"I guess you'd need an incinerator," I said, thought. "And it would have to be big incinerator. With a wide door."

"Yes."

"And moving the body is a problem itself, right?"

"That's right."

"And there's probably no way we have access to an incinerator you could fit a whole giraffe in anyway."

"Correct."

"So we ship it out? Someone comes to get it to use, I don't know, the bones."

"It stays here," said Doc. "You're getting there."

"I'm stuck now."

"Here's your problem—you look at an animal. You look at a body. You think it's one thing. You think it's an idea. But it's a body."

"You cut it up?"

"It's the only way."

"You have to use a chainsaw, don't you?" I said. Doc nodded. "The chainsaw I used to cut up fallen tree branches."

"You got there."

"That's terrible."

"It's not terrible," said Doc. "It's not good. It's the way."

When I told Caroline I was calling in sick on her day off to take her to brunch at the restaurant at the top of the Devon tower downtown, she was not as appreciative as I had expected.

"Who wants to eat in the sky?" she said.

"It'll be cool," I said. "Believe me."

"I don't have anything to wear," she said.

When she picked me up she was wearing a sundress patterned in dandelions and bright red lipstick and she'd done her hair in a shockingly intricate swooping wave, pinned up and over on one side of her head.

"You look good," I said.

"Thanks," she said.

"I don't know if I've ever seen the inside of your ear before," I said, like I'd say anything, but her hand flew up to cover her ear.

"Is it bad?" she said. "Should I change?"

"No," I said, saw what I had done. "I didn't mean to make you self-conscious."

"Then don't," she said.

We parked in the garage and emerged from the garage elevator into the luxurious expanse of the tower corporate lobby. Abstract glass chandeliers dangled above us like stunned angels.

We walked along the long murmuring indoor reflective pool to get to the restaurant's dedicated pair of silver elevators.

Caroline was unusually quiet.

The elevator only had two buttons. We rose frictionless up and up in the blind box. When the doors opened, the restaurant was immediately bright, the high clear yellow light of an Oklahoma summer blazing through windows tinted just shy of blinding.

It had been a few months since I'd been in a space like that, but I was comfortable; the tablecloths were a luxurious ironed white, the silverware was laid with gleaming precision, and the gray-suited men and news-anchor-suited women were the sort of people my father was perhaps having brunch with at that very moment. I felt a sort of assurance; this world was still open to me, even if I had the previous day accidentally smeared my cheek with hyena shit.

I turned to Caroline, to take her hand, to complete the picture, but she was gone.

There she was, on the other side of the bar, standing between two tables full of women with salads and glasses of white wine. She was a dark silhouette cut out of the obliterating light of the day. As I watched she leaned forward slightly; she rested her forehead directly on the glass.

One of the brunching women turned to eye the intrusion.

I joined Caroline.

"You know," I said quietly, "we'll be able to see out the window from our table."

"Look," she said.

Oklahoma spread out forever in every direction, yellow and green and flat and dry. The highways from this height were part of the land, not merely paths across it. There were birds in the air below us.

I took Caroline's hand, tugged her gently away, but she didn't move.

"Look," she said.

"Let's eat," I said.

"I can't believe we're up here," she said.

"It's a restaurant," I said. "Anyone can be here."

"Sir?" said a voice behind me; I turned and it was the waiter, a slim dark-haired man, looking at me in a slightly tilted-down way that a waiter had never looked at me before.

"One moment," I said, too loudly, and the waiter's expression didn't change. We appraised each other. I could have pulled again at Caroline's hand, but I did not; I held it.

Caroline then lifted her face from the window and turned half to me.

"I feel drunk," she said with an odd gentleness, like she was falling asleep. I smiled at the waiter, who did not smile, but nodded, and withdrew.

I ordered for both of us the Mexican white chocolate pancakes with tangerine foam. Caroline held her jewel-cut water glass in the air between us, to see and show how it fractured and collected the sunlight.

The week after I surprised Doc's friend by the dumpsters, there was another animal missing, a venomous green tree viper.

But it was just a snake. There was no morning meeting. Even Maggie didn't seem anxious about it.

"I don't get snakes," she said as we were raking nibbled shards of limp lettuce out of the porcupine's enclosure. "They spook me, the way they move. I feel bad about it."

"You feel bad about not liking snakes? I don't really like them either. I'm sure they don't mind."

"You'd be surprised what they can understand. My friend once had a snake who knew his voice and who'd sleep in his lap."

"Okay," I said.

But before my lunch break Maggie got a crackly-blast on the walkie-talkie to send me in to see Dr. Colcord. I was more annoyed than worried. I assumed he just wanted to talk again. To give me some advice. He was not the opposite of my father.

This time his office door was open and he wasn't looking at the computer or at anything on his desk. He'd been waiting for me.

"Are you a student of animal psychology?" said Dr. Colcord, not even saying hello.

"Yes, but not formally," I said sitting down. He smiled. I suspected he was used to knowing more about any topic of discussion than whomever he was speaking with, and he enjoyed the imbalance.

"Then you've come across the term 'Umwelt'?"

"Not exactly," I said. He nodded as I answered, expecting it.

"It's a German word meaning, more or less, 'world view.' The idea is that each animal experiences the world, sees the world, in a different way, depending on its sensory organs, its biological needs, its abilities. Each animal has its own umwelt. Are you with me?"

"Sure," I said. "Makes sense."

"I think it's useful to think about human life in the same way. How we understand the world and how we move within it depends on where we start from. What our values are. What our goals are."

"Okay."

"Now, it's clear that your goals and your potential are larger than most people your age. You want more out of life than selling stuffed animals at a gift shop." Caroline was at that second probably staring a shelf of rat-sized tigers. I considered.

"I want to be a good person," I said.

"A good person, yes. An effective person. I'm glad to hear it," he said. "Now, you're probably wondering what I'm getting at."

"I am."

"It has to do with the recent thefts."

"I'd never steal anything in a million years," I couldn't stop myself from saying. And it was true. I couldn't imagine a reason powerful enough to make me steal. Dr. Colcord smiled.

"We wouldn't be having this conversation if I thought you would," he said. "Quite the opposite: I'm actually suggesting that we share an umwelt, a sense of the universal value of justice and a sense of our responsibility to uphold it. Because how can any institution function without justice?" I didn't know what to say. "What I say now can't leave this room," he said. I said nothing. "Now, we don't know how the most recent abduction happened. But we know where it happened."

"How do you know?"

"You already know that we've been increasing security. But what you don't know is that, since the last incident, we've significantly expanded our surveillance systems in ways I'm not at liberty to discuss. The upshot of all this is we were able to capture some meaningful, though fragmentary, information."

"What did you see?" I said.

"What's important for you to know is that the animal was removed during the afternoon hours, and traveled through the animal hospital. What happened happened during normal zoo operations."

"Okay."

"So you see how you are in a unique position, with a unique opportunity to assist in the pursuit of justice."

"Because whoever did it must have been someone who works in the hospital building during the day. Like me."

"Exactly," he said. "Now, all I'm asking is for you to keep your values in mind and to keep your eyes open. And remember that work for justice is always rewarded."

"What reward?" I said. Dr. Colcord smiled.

"You'll understand as you grow into this life that you shouldn't ask that question out loud. That's the umwelt. You'll be able to look at another person, and know who they are, and understand what they can do for you. There's more power in the acknowledgment of shared values than there is in any physical transaction."

I left his office and found myself composing my face as I reentered the world. I understood how I would be expected to behave with such knowledge.

Immediately upon stepping out into the wet crowded heat of the zoo and the world, I was visited by a flash of insight: Doc had stolen the animals.

I didn't know anything about Doc: where he lived, what kind of car he drove. He was always at work when I got there and was always there when I left. He was not like Maggie; he didn't care for animals with a sense of wonder, or even affection. But he always knew what to do to keep them healthy.

Stealing animals would be a simple enough operation, if you knew as much about animals as he did, if you had access to what pills and potions that he did. He knew what every animal needed to eat, what every atypical behavior meant, why that giraffe we got from Baltimore was always gnawing on the hand rail. The garbage truck was the obvious method of sneaking out a concealed animal. All you had to do was understand that hiding a living creature in garbage was odd, not impossible; garbage was just objects, pieces of the world.

I wasn't exactly sure what his purpose in stealing the animals was. It wasn't impossible to imagine him selling them. He would know what an animal was worth, who would pay, how to keep them alive until then.

Later that afternoon he told me again I didn't know how to use a shovel, and then he again showed me his way, sliding the bucket of the shovel as flat along the earth as he could. "It's like a spoon," he told me. "You know not to stab soup, I hope."

I didn't like Doc, exactly, but I knew I wouldn't turn him in. His life was his life, and my life was my life, and I didn't need any reward.

All I wanted was to see proof, the thing itself, the truth.

The path through the Big Cat Forest comes out along the murky lake that borders the zoo to the east. Against the fence there is a quarter candy machine that seems at first to hold nuts, little pellets of some kind. There is no sign. There are some ducks drifting near shore. The machine is selling dog food, you understand. You turn the quarter for the handful of pellets, toss some in for the ducks and only then do you see the turtles rising up to the surface of the water like hard bubbles, and then below your feet the edge of the lake boils with ravenous catfish.

Caroline and I were sitting on my front steps on a Friday night. It was past midnight but there were still people out, stumblers and couples coming back from the bars. The light from streetlamps seemed to hover, like stuck hazy clouds. I'd always hated heat, but Caroline never seemed to mind, so I'd been trying to not mind and sometimes succeeding. I was wondering what it means about our ability to grasp the real world if it is possible to consciously adjust how we receive sensory information. Does that mean we can really only see and experience what we intend to see and experience? Or does it mean that we can think of perception like a grimy window we can remind ourselves to wipe clear?

I explained what I was thinking to Caroline.

"I guess," she said.

"No," I said. "Really. What do you think?"

"I think it doesn't matter. If you're standing on the train tracks and there's a train coming, it doesn't matter if you see the train or if you know what a train is or if you think the train is happy or sad. The train is coming. It just is."

"That's an extreme example," I said.

"Not if you don't want to get hit by a train."

Later we walked through black oily heat to the convenience store for Dr. Peppers. I told her about how I'd had a staring contest with a gorilla and lost. She told me when she was a child, she'd gotten caught in a riptide at a beach on the Texas coast and pulled way out. She hadn't been afraid. She knew to stay calm, swim not against the pull but parallel to the shore, until you were free.

"What happens when summer ends?" said Caroline.

"It's not over yet," I said.

"You're in denial. There's less than two weeks. Ten days."

"Two-hundred and forty hours, then," I said, looking up into the ceiling of the sky. "If I counted every second, that would feel like forever."

I had always watched Doc carefully because he knew how to do everything. He was a normal-sized man, but his hands were unusually long-fingered and knobby, good tools. He was also like some animals in the zoo in that he did not seem to notice being stared at.

After I understood that he was the secret animal thief, I paid even closer attention.

In the room where we signed out walkie-talkies, there was a mailbox with slots for full-time keepers. It was not for me. But one day I came in and Doc was of course there, and he had opened a letter and was frowning and reading it. It was nothing unusual, plastic window in the envelope, maybe financial forms, something from the adult world. What was strange was that, when he folded the letter and slipped it back in the envelope, finished reading, he didn't drop it in the giant blue recycling bin on the floor at his feet, as anyone would have, but he tore it, quickly, in half once, then twice, and then he carried the torn pieces with him, past a trash can, out of the mail room into the hall.

Maybe he was being sensibly protective, but it seemed to me paranoid, an awareness of guilt. I ducked into the hall in time to see him push open the door and then shove his crumpled paper into the first trash can along the path outside.

It was still early; the public was still in the parking lot, in line at the ticket booth. I waited until I knew Doc was gone and went out to the trash.

It smelled like hot diapers.

But I reached in, fished out the papers. I didn't know what I was looking for. Maybe a letter about an agreement to purchase a stolen monkey. It turned out to be an update about changes to the dental plan. Boilerplate language, charts of numbers and names. Nothing. But then I saw it: his home address.

"He lives out there?" said Caroline when I showed her.

"Why?" I said. "What does that mean?"

"That's out *out* there. He must have some land."

"If you're taking care of animals to sell, you need space and you don't want nosy neighbors, right?"

"You act like you saw him stuff an iguana into his pants. How can you be so sure?"

"You don't work with him. You don't know what he's like," I said. I saw it came out like an insult.

"No," she said.

"We could go see," I said.

"What, like perform surveillance? Like spies?"

"If you want to call it that," I said.

"I've done dumber things," she said.

"Like what?" I said.

"Wouldn't you like to know," she said.

We bolted when work let out. I knew Doc was still working because he'd been helping the vets draw blood from the giraffes that afternoon and had had quite a bit to say about how to position the needles and how it was taking too much time. When I left he was chewing on the side of his tongue, his hands resting on his hips, looking into the cage of a listless African painted dog that had been brought into the animal hospital for observation; he had the aura of a man with an infinite amount of work ahead of him.

We drove North and East. Oklahoma City goes on forever in certain directions—you can drive in a straight line for miles and miles and pass 300 roofs that look exactly the same, all hidden behind the same brick wall. In other directions, you can zip through a stoplight past an office park and end up on a two-lane road in rolling prairie, clumps of trees in hollows, grazing horses fenced-in by barbed wire.

Doc's address, it became clear, was indeed far out; the cross streets were narrow crumbled pavement, went out endlessly in either direction. We were the only car on the road.

"We probably should have thought about how not to be seen," I said.

"He lives near an intersection," said Caroline. "We'll drive past the property so he won't see us if he gets out of work early. And we'll park on the cross street and see what we can see from there. Plus he doesn't even know what my car looks like. Plus we probably won't see anything."

"You've done this before."

"No," she said. "I just thought it through."

"You still think this is stupid?"

"I like being out here," she said. It was an ideal summer early evening. Hot as usual, but clear, and less humid, a huge sky with scattered bright cotton ball clouds. The grassy fields were not all completely yellow. "Sometimes I think I could just drop out of school and find somewhere out here where I could just drive a tractor or herd goats or whatever all day."

"You'd get lonely," I said.

"You can get lonely anywhere," she said.

We entered a patch of woods, ditches and dense undergrowth to the right, and then there was Doc's address, an ordinary black metal mailbox, a closed gate (of the sort you had to physically lift and move to open), a gravel drive curling up through trees to a long low house, a not-enormous-or-shiny black pickup in the driveway and another building, a white barn.

Caroline rolled through the stop sign and turned right onto another thin endless road. Here the shoulder was almost nonexistent, but the land was flat enough before dipping down into a long wooded ditch along one side. On the other side of the ditch, halfway up a rise I couldn't see over, I could make out a barbed wire fence flagged with metal signs that said "PRIVATE PROPERTY."

"Seems like he's trying to hide something," I said.

"Or he's like every other old guy in Oklahoma," she said. "He probably just put up those signs so he has a good excuse to shoot anyone who comes onto his land."

"It doesn't matter," I said. "He's at work still."

"So who's truck is that?"

"It's his," I said. "Got to be. He's probably got two. There's no way he could live with another person."

"You know for sure?"

"I don't," I said. "But I know."

"You're totally set on going in? You want to see that bad?"

"You can stay in the car," I said.

"I should," she said. "What are you planning on doing, if he's the one?"

"I just wanna see," I said.

"I should stay here," she said.

"Come with me," I said.

It was Caroline's idea to write "Out of Gas" on an envelope and stick it under a windshield wiper, in case anyone came by.

It was so quiet I could hear grasshoppers popping into the air like matches catching fire.

I wasn't exactly nervous; I was so sure of what I wanted to see, I wasn't thinking through the consequences. The ditch was dried mud; in the spring, it was probably wet and green. We ducked through the fence; insects zzzed in the trees above us. Caroline, just behind me, was watching her feet as she walked.

"I stepped on a snake once," she said.

"Shh," I said.

"Talking quietly is not going to blow our cover," she said.

We made our way up the little hill and I held Caroline's hand, to make sure we took the last few steps slowly, as if she'd run ahead.

We came to the top of the rise and I ducked behind a cottonwood. Caroline stood a bit back, did not hide. "You can see fine from here," she said.

From where I stood, half-hidden, I could see the side of the white barn and behind that cleared land, and arrayed in the shade were substantial chainlink cages, a large fenced in lot. What I saw first was the pronghorn antelope, the same as we had at the zoo, grazing, head down, oblivious of everything but the grass; it took some looking, but I could see the other, the younger one, the one that had been stolen several weeks ago, with its nose in a pile of tossed hay, not far away.

Some kind of monkey in one of the tall cages came to life and swooped down from a hanging rope.

"I knew it," I said, and then I turned back to Caroline, and she was looking past me at the antelope and the cages and the compound with a look on her face that was not surprise or wonder, but like she was disappointed.

"We should go," she said.

"Isn't this incredible?" I said. "And look how many cages there are!" I thought, and turned away from Caroline. "He's not selling them. He's living with them. It's, like, his private zoo." A few seconds later a door in the white outbuilding opened and out of it came not Doc, but another man in a khaki work jumpsuit, with a white bucket full of what looked like lettuce. It took me a moment to recognize the garbage truck driver.

He could have been a lover, or a friend, or a son— the fact that Doc had been stealing animals was less surprising than the idea that Doc let anyone enter his home, period.

The world was so much more than what it appeared to be.

I ducked and backed away, slowly. Caroline was already halfway down the hill.

"Did you see that?" I said.

"I did," she said.

On our first day tour, us new interns were taken into the animal hospital. Inside was like a doctor's office except that the doorways were wider and some of the rooms were not sized for human proportions and so slightly nightmarish. There were sinks and soap dispensers, glass cabinets full of vials and bottles, rolling metal tables, movable operating lights attached to great robot arms, the smell of bleach. We were taken into one of the operating rooms. It had been built to allow zoo visitors to watch certain procedures, so the room was tall and at the top there were windows, looking down from an observation room. That day there were a handful of people up there, a mother with a child on each side of her, watching. It was the first moment I felt like I was on the inside, that I was somewhere new, somewhere real.

Two sky-blue latex-gloved keepers were treating a road runner—a stretched out speckled brown pheasant—who had abraded her chin and throat by, we were told, continuously rubbing it against a concrete corner in her enclosure, either as a response to an insect bite, or infection, or because of a garbled instinctual response to living in confinement. One keeper was standing at a small table in the center of the room with one hand around the bird's chest and another on its long neck, keeping the needle of the bird's beak pointed straight up, holding her still. The bird was awake, spooked and still at the same time in a way only a bird can be. It was easy to see that the flesh of the bird's neck, beneath the layer of white feathers, was inflamed. The other keeper, one hand resting around the base of the bird's neck in a loose ring, brushed the affected area gently, as with a little finger, with what looked like a Q-tip; every so often she dipped the Q-tip into what looked like a cup of white foam.

Everyone was very quiet. An atmosphere of eerie professional tenderness.

After, we went into the necropsy room. It was colder. The other summer interns crowded around a dead zebra, eagerly leaning in close to observe, as if it was the same.

The morning after our trip out to Doc's ranch, I was woken up by a fat man standing in my bedroom doorway.

"Who the hell are you?" he said.

It was the landlord. It turned out the lease would be over the next weekend, earlier than I'd thought.

It was no longer possible to not acknowledge the summer would end. It was not only Tuesday morning; it was the last Tuesday morning. On Saturday I'd be gone. In a week I'd be back in Dallas in a tastefully wallpapered room at my father's firm, sitting at a shiny heavy table performing whatever manila-foldered task had been set before me, wearing a tie, living in the agreed-upon future.

On my bike ride to work, I kept forgetting to stay alert to the wind and the world. I thought, "what does it even matter that I figured out who stole all the animals. In a week it will matter to no one in my life." I found myself gliding through the parking lot, thinking "there's no point in thinking about where you'll be next week," and "stop thinking that you're thinking."

In the zoo on my way to meet Maggie at the bears, I stopped for a moment outside the lion overlook. Prince wasn't doing anything, just sitting on the platform, facing away. I made myself stop and consider. A real lion is so different from a picture of a lion, from the idea of a lion. It's only flesh and blood. It's a yellow hairy stupid giant cat. What was I doing with my life? I had seen and touched many strange animals that summer, smelled terrible smells. I couldn't say what I had gained. But I knew I would miss the zoo. That seemed like a meager result.

I didn't notice Dr. Colcord until he was standing directly next to me, facing the placid lion through the glass.

"We almost had to send that male to San Antonio," he said.

"Why?" I said.

"The short answer is we had a major donor who had a sudden shift in priorities."

"What's the long answer?"

"The long answer is the rest of the world. Oil fields in North Dakota. Questionable investments into research and development of horizontal drilling technologies. Bad accounting. The Saudis' whims, a hurricane amplifying a turn in the market."

"The sun and the moon?" I said.

"You could make that argument if you wanted to."

"So how did you keep him?"

"If everything is connected, as I've always believed, it's necessary to understand how things are connected and how power flows through those connections. More simply, you have to know how to ask the right questions, and of whom, and at the right moment."

It was his life I was destined for.

"Did you ever actually want to be a zookeeper?" I said.

"When I was very young," he said.

"I never did," I said.

"I didn't think so," he said. "I see a lot of myself in you." He meant it as a compliment; it was not. I tried not to hear it.

"Don't get me wrong," I said. "I'm grateful to be here. But I know I'm not good at taking care of animals. I don't have enough of a sense of what an animal really needs. And I don't think I could dedicate my whole self to it. There's a difference in someone who you know is

120

a zookeeper. Like Maggie. She loves animals. And Doc. He knows them."

Dr. Colcord nodded.

"Even though your position here has always been temporary, I know it couldn't have been an easy thing to do," he said. "But the best move isn't always the easiest move."

I didn't know what he meant right away; I almost asked what he was talking about, but I didn't. Later, I saw how smart I had been, how well I'd subconsciously picked up on his tone: there was something behind it he assumed I agreed with, something that would be vulgar to say out loud. It was not the first time I'd been strategically quiet. I again seemed to know instinctively to never show confusion in certain situations, to keep an impassive facade. I was not proud of myself.

"Sure," I said and watched Prince not care about a fox squirrel dashing across his line of sight.

"To be honest," Dr. Colcord told me then, "I was surprised you let your girlfriend claim the reward. In the future," he said, smiling, obviously pleased with his own good advice, "take every opportunity to take the lead."

I knew instantly it was true: Caroline had told him where the disappeared animals lived. And she'd already asked about reward money.

"You found all the animals?" I said and bit the inside of my cheek.

"We've recovered all of the stolen property, yes. Most of it will be easy enough to reintegrate into the zoo population. They were cared for more than competently. I'll say that for him."

"What are you going to do to him?"

"Well, we're not the police. And the animals are returned in acceptable health. So we'll decline to press charges. He was immediately fired, of course."

"You had to fire him?"

"Of course! Think about it. What would the consequences be of letting him remain here?"

"Healthy wallabies."

"Empty exhibits," he said. "And what good would my word be then?"

"I don't need any of the reward," I said. "You can give it all to Caroline."

"That's up to you," he said. "But I can appreciate the gesture. It's clear you understand there are some things more valuable than money."

"Right," I said.

When I caught up to Maggie outside the bears, she wrapped me up in a full body hug and squeezed me hard. She was strong, and smelled like soap.

"Did you hear?" she said. "Did you hear?"

Midmorning, checking on the pregnant warthog, she looked up with tears in her eyes.

"What's wrong?" I said.

"I just can't believe they're coming home," she said.

"Can you believe it was Doc?"

"I'll believe anything you tell me about a person," she said.

Caroline was supposed to be at the gift shop, but when I got there on my break, behind the register was an unfamiliar older woman who looked like a prairie dog with tight curled gray hair.

Caroline read but did not respond to my texts.

After work I biked to her house. The neighborhood felt different in the daylight—quieter, like life was elsewhere.

Her car wasn't on the street but there was another car, an older silver Camry, parked in front of her house. I knocked on the front door and it was opened into darkness by a woman, Caroline's mother, it was obvious, in the set of her mouth and something about her eyes. She held the door handle a little too tightly. As she leaned into the light I could see that her hair was frazzled and her forehead was dotted with sweat, like she'd just returned from a run, though she was wearing jeans and a cardigan sweater. She looked not just surprised but scared.

"Yes?" she said.

"I'm looking for Caroline," I said. "I know her from the zoo."

"You must be her young man," she said.

"I suppose so."

"I'll tell her you stopped by," she said, but stood there searching my face. Something was wrong.

"Is it her brother?" I said.

"I'm sorry," she said. "We have to go." And she closed the door.

I got on my bike. Stay pointed away from downtown in a certain direction and soon enough you are on a long straight road through where the grass and the horizon and the sky are constants. Flying, but only flying in place. And it's starting to get dark, it's not summer anymore and you are far away from the place where you sleep.

I turned around.

On the ride back, I thought about Doc. I was sure he'd been up before dawn every morning, to feed and water the animals. The uncertain young pronghorn. Maybe he didn't speak warmly to them. But he saw them. Cared for them. He shouldn't have taken them, but he did. What had he felt those million dark mornings to wake up amid the rustling of all those creatures stirring? What would he feel now when he woke in dark stillness?

Something was over. There was no value, I knew, in even bothering to finish the week at the zoo.

By the time I got back to the apartment, it was

123

dark and I was exhausted. I could have fallen asleep on the sidewalk. The future was laid out in front of me, like a book of maps. All I had to do was let the night turn the page.

Instead, I pedaled away.

It was dark enough to be dangerous; the bike lights' batteries were dead. I turned on my phone's flashlight and jammed it into my shoe, to make a bright wobbling warning to cars.

The air was thick but slightly cooler than it had been, like breathing through wet cloth. It didn't matter whether my eyes were open or not. I kept going and kept going. It was like I would be on my bike all night but then, there was Caroline, sitting on her front steps, a face glowing in the light of her phone.

I knew right away I wasn't angry at her. I was sad.

She was wearing a windbreaker and jeans. I hadn't seen her in pants all summer. Hospitals, I knew, were well air-conditioned.

She looked up when she heard the bike and snapped off her phone and her face blinked out.

I stayed on my bike.

"I stopped by earlier," I said.

"I know," she said.

"You could have asked me," I said.

"Would it have mattered?"

"No," I said.

"See?"

"He was taking just as good care of those animals as they do at the zoo," I said. "Better care."

"He broke the law."

"So what?" I said. "He wasn't bothering anyone."

"Don't you think I know that?" she said. I laid the bike on the ground and sat on the step beside her.

"It's your brother, isn't it?" I said.

"What do you think?"

"I thought you said money can't do anything?"

"It can't do everything. It can do some things. And don't worry," she said, spitting it out. "I didn't say it was all mine. You'll get what's yours."

"I don't want it," I said. I couldn't see her face well in the dark, only her profile. She wasn't looking at me. She looked ready to fight the air. "You should have it," I said.

We sat there together in the dark.

"Is he going to die?" I said after awhile.

"I don't know," she said.

"This is kind of a fucked-up way for the summer to end," I said. "I wish it wasn't like this."

"There's no point in wishing," she said.

"I don't want it to be over," I said. "I don't want to say goodbye."

"You know," said Caroline, "it's not like you're moving to the moon. You can come back on weekends. You only have to say goodbye if you're actually saying goodbye."

A moment of quiet bloomed. No usual ambient hum of nearby traffic. It was the kind of pure shocking quiet only possible in cities because it was rare and unpredictable. We were not separated by the quiet but inside of it together.

"I'm not saying goodbye," I said.

My phone buzzed on my last Wednesday lunch break and it was my college friend Bryce trying to Facetime. I would never have answered, so I answered.

There was his face. He was wearing a suit, and his hair was different, oddly stiff and shiny. He was standing outside—behind him, the windows of skyscrapers, clouds and sky. He was on some rooftop in New York.

"Bro," he said, his lips curling slightly into his new smirk, probably the face he had become used to showing the world.

"Hey, man," I said. "What's going on? Where are you right now"

"Check this shit out," he said, and lifted his phone. He tapped on his screen, intending to switch the camera so I could see what he was seeing, but he did something wrong and my perspective didn't change and he didn't notice, so I kept seeing his face. His eyes went wide and his mouth hung open as he looked out in plain dopey wonder at what must have been a panorama of the great city seen from a great height, all those lines and colors and human lives.

"Cool," I said. "Awesome."

My last Thursday was as normal a day as it could have been.

The usual chores, the usual heat, the tiger pacing the worn path around the boundary of his enclosure. I tried to memorize the face of the elderly tortoise.

After work, I biked to Doc's property. It looked the same. The gate was closed. I could see the long low building, the white barn I knew was now empty of life. The only car in the driveway was a dusty white pickup. He was home.

I left my bike by the gate. I was halfway up the gravel driveway when I decided to turn back and, in the same instant, saw Doc watching me from a lawn chair in a patch of shadow, camouflaged by his stillness.

I stopped in front of him, about as close as a zoo visitor can get to a rhinoceros. He was not exactly looking at me.

"You're already trespassing," he said. "I'm not writing out a formal invitation."

I took five more steps. He was wearing the same flat gray work pants he wore at the zoo but on top only a stretched-out white T-shirt. He was holding an empty glass that looked like it had been empty for some time. All I could do was say what I had come to say.

"I came to say I'm sorry," I said.

"That doesn't mean anything to me," he said.

"I didn't mean for this happen," I said. He finally looked at me.

"I can't absolve you of your sins, kid. You gotta live with who you are same as everyone else does." I waited. I had the sense that I could have waited there forever without him ever speaking another word.

"Why'd you do it?" I said.

"I knew what those animals needed," he said.

"I thought maybe you were selling them," I said.

He closed his eyes and shook his head side to side slowly, once. I have never been more ashamed of myself.

"Kid," he said.

"I'm sorry," I said.

"I liked having them close by," he said. He opened his eyes. He wasn't looking at me. "I'll say it. I liked them here. Simple as that." He paused, took a gulp from his empty glass, looked into it. "I knew it wouldn't last forever."

A stingray's back is soft and firm and slimy.

The best way to measure the length of a snake is to photocopy it and measure the copy.

River otters undulate botanically underwater.

A wild boar sniffs the dirt exactly like my childhood dog.

The rhinoceros moves with the armored lack of grace of a robot made out of a washing machine.

The porcupine sleeps like a pile of rotten wood with nails sticking out.

The elk has a tree growing up through its skull.

Even the anaconda needs a wellness exam; even the crickets need to be fed; even the fish need water; even the gorillas need quiet.

Vipers sleep resting their jaws on the hammocks of their own bodies.

The mesa foxes sit facing the exact same direction, their faces like living resting knives.

A whitetail deer is a dream a cow has about itself.

The bats hang from the ceiling like tiny hairy grenades.

The cougar's paws are heavy and soft.

Meerkats are altruistic.

Elephants have more hair than they did in my imagination.

The barn owl sees you before you see her.

It always appears at first that the black widow's window is empty.

Some tree frogs are so bright they can't be real, but they are.

I don't know what any of this means.

On my last morning I got to observe a bison eye procedure inside the animal hospital. She had developed some kind of infection inside her eyelid. I first had to help four or five keepers roll the woozy enormous creature onto a trailer to be pulled behind a pickup, then I had to walk carefully alongside it on the way to the hospital. One of the keepers kept his hand on the shaggy creature's shoulder the entire way. We were like a parade moving through a late August Oklahoma morning. It felt dignified, ceremonial. No one was watching us.

In the hospital we had to roll her up onto a table. It was difficult, like lifting a breathing car that smelled liked wet grass. It's very rare in life that you have to strain so much while also trying to remain gentle.

I couldn't see much of the procedure from where I was standing. There were many people in the room—keepers and interns—and soon enough the general public appeared above us in the observation windows. Though I could not see her hands, I watched the veterinary surgeon's face. She was completely absorbed in her task.

I wondered what it would be like to be an animal, sick or hurt, to drift into sleep and then wake up somewhere unfamiliar, sore but stitched together, healed. The bison would have no memory of the surgeon—the hands that had healed her—but she would be healed.

I was finished with the zoo; I was not finished with the world.

That afternoon I packed my bags in preparation for my father's arrival. Then I biked to Caroline's house, but she didn't want to be there or at the hospital, so I offered to drive her car to Lake Hefner just northwest of the city. We drove around the lake and didn't stop driving around it as the sun was setting. After spending so much time on my bike, driving in a car felt oddly frictionless. Lake Hefner is small and man-made; the length of one side is traced by a busy highway. There were sailboats on the water; the sky was clear as the water. I didn't know what to say; I told her about Doc; I told her about the bison's operation. I didn't know what would happen between us, I only knew that I wanted to be with her and that I was with her.

The earth became dark, then the sky. We went around and around and around. She was thinking about the way the surgeon had worked on the bison's eye. It became clear to me that the shoreline of any lake is infinite. The difference between a moment and eternity is only a matter of degree. Every newborn kangaroo is more alive than all the stars.

About the author

Rob Roensch is the author of *The Wildflowers of Baltimore*, winner of The International Scott Prize for Short Stories, published by Salt Publishing in 2012. He has published short fiction in *American Short Fiction*, *Epoch* and elsewhere. He lives in Oklahoma City with his wife and two daughters.